He was her worst nightmare.
He was her hottest fantasy.

And he was standing in Aunt Stella's driveway!

Laurel had tried to forget Wade Taggart—nearly
had, in fact. But Lord, he looked good—and
dangerous.

"Wh-what are you doing here?" she asked,
mortified at the croaking sound she emitted.

"I could ask you the same question, Princess," he
said, insolence dripping from each word. "Did
you come to kiss me goodbye?"

"Kiss?" She'd ice-skate in hell before doing that
again. "Where are you going?"

Then she knew. Wade Taggart intended to go with
her and Aunt Stella on her honeymoon quest!

Dear Reader,

What makes a man a SUPER FABULOUS FATHER? In bestselling author Lindsay Longford's *Undercover Daddy*, detective Walker Ford promises to protect a little boy with his life. Even though that means an undercover marriage to the child's mother—the woman he'd always loved but could never have...until now.

Book 2 of Silhouette's cross-line continuity miniseries, DADDY KNOWS LAST, continues with *Baby in a Basket* by award-winning author Helen R. Myers. A confirmed bachelor finds a baby on his doorstep—with a note claiming the baby is his!

In Carolyn Zane's *Marriage in a Bottle*, a woman is granted seven wishes by a very mysterious, very sexy stranger. And her greatest wish is to make him her husband....

How is a woman to win over a bachelor cowboy and his three protective little cowpokes? With lots of love—in *Cowboy at the Wedding* by Karen Rose Smith, book one of her new miniseries, THE BEST MEN.

Why does Laurel suddenly want to say "I do" to the insufferable—irresistible—man who broke her heart long ago? It's all in *The Honeymoon Quest* by Dana Lindsey.

All Tip wants is to be with single dad Rob Winfield and his baby daughter, but will her past catch up with her? Don't miss *Mommy for the Moment* by Lisa Kaye Laurel.

From classic love stories to romantic comedies to emotional heart tuggers, Silhouette Romance brings you six irresistible novels this month—and every month—by six talented authors. I hope you treasure each and every one.

Regards,

Melissa Senate
Senior Editor

Please address questions and book requests to:
Silhouette Reader Service
U.S.: 3010 Walden Ave., P.O. Box 1325, Buffalo, NY 14269
Canadian: P.O. Box 609, Fort Erie, Ont. L2A 5X3

THE HONEYMOON QUEST

Dana Lindsey

Silhouette

ROMANCE™

Published by Silhouette Books

America's Publisher of Contemporary Romance

For Jodi O'Donnell Raynor, good friend, insightful critic; for all you do, this book's for you; and

For Charlie Brown, who persists, thank goodness, in loving and pampering a romance writer, even when she's semi-irascible; and

In memory of a certain unlamented, unreliable car that inspired parts of this book.

 SILHOUETTE BOOKS

ISBN 0-373-19172-3

THE HONEYMOON QUEST

Copyright © 1996 by Dora M. Brown

Printed in U.S.A.

Books by Dana Lindsey

Silhouette Romance

Julie's Garden #1071
The Honeymoon Quest #1172

DANA LINDSEY

loves to travel on the knees of comfort, if not in the lap of luxury. She's visited all the places mentioned in *The Honeymoon Quest*, most of them in the heat of the summer. To Dana, an air-conditioned reliable car is one of God's finest gifts to humankind.

When they aren't traveling, Dana and her husband live in Dallas, where they plan their next adventure.

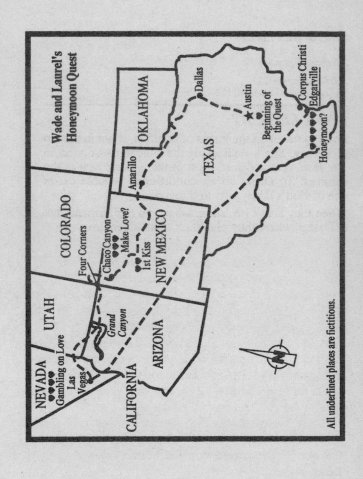

Wade and Laurel's Honeymoon Quest

NEVADA

UTAH

Gambling on Love

Las Vegas

COLORADO

Four Corners

Chaco Canyon

Make Love?

1st Kiss

Grand Canyon

NEW MEXICO

ARIZONA

CALIFORNIA

OKLAHOMA

Dallas

Amarillo

TEXAS

Austin

Beginning of the Quest

Corpus Christi

Edgarville

Honeymoon?

N

All underlined places are fictitious.

Chapter One

"There won't be enough room," Stella Martin insisted staunchly, patting her faded red hair.

"Of course there will be, Aunt Stella," Laurel Covington said patiently, assuring her great-aunt for the third time. "We're going to put the ice chest in the back seat and our suitcases in the trunk. There will be plenty of space, since we aren't taking anything else. Oh, except the urn with Uncle Homer's ashes." How could she have forgotten the ashes, the whole reason for this trip?

"But, what about...?" Stella set her capacious handbag on the driveway. "Hmm. Maybe I forgot to tell you?" She squinted, then blinked slowly several times.

"What?" Laurel asked, concerned about her beloved aunt's confusion that had seemed especially worrisome since Laurel's arrival this morning. Seeing Stella's deterioration had made her question the wisdom of this "quest," as her aunt had dubbed what was to be their jaunt to who-knew-where. Conversely, observing her condition also made Laurel more determined that this last fling, so to speak, would be everything the old dear wanted it to be.

Absently Stella tugged at the front of her shabby housedress, but the halfhearted effort to cool herself was useless, for the July noontime sun baked Austin, Texas, like a tortilla.

"Perhaps we should put off this trip until you're up to it," Laurel said gently. "We don't have to go while it's so hot."

"But we can't do that. It's all planned out. Everyone's on their way."

The growl of a motor grew louder, interrupting their conversation. In seconds a battered sports car, its rusty color reminiscent of dried blood, roared into Stella's driveway and screeched to a halt, tainting the air with the acrid scents of exhaust and burning rubber.

The driver of the ancient convertible wore a wide-brimmed Australian bush hat and a black T-shirt stretched over broad shoulders and a lean, muscular torso. Danger emanated from him like radiant heat. The raw power of man and machine aroused a slow, warm throbbing deep inside Laurel.

Overpowering.

Instinctively she stepped back, grasping Stella's frail arm protectively.

He gunned the engine to an ear-splitting howl, then eased off the gas, his face concealed by the shade of his hat brim. He switched off the engine and in the sudden silence hoisted himself up, stepped over the low-slung door and strode toward them, the rhythmic slap of his scuffed black boots against the pavement the only sound.

Laurel's skin prickled, and the fine hairs at her nape stood on end. Who was he? What did he want? She could sense the man appraising them through mirrored sunglasses. She sucked in a breath, preparing to stand her ground.

"Wade, darling!" Stella crowed. Shaking free of Laurel's hold, she scurried into the man's arms. "It's about time you got here."

Wade? Wade Taggart? Dear God!

He pulled off his sunglasses, bent down and wrapped Stella in a bear hug.

"How's the love of my life?" The words rumbled from deep in his chest as he clasped her. With a kiss on the top of her head, he held her gently against his side, as though she were made of fine porcelain, then shot a glance at Laurel.

She glimpsed his eyes, so dark she couldn't distinguish iris from pupil. Eyes that again held her captive after twelve years, then he covered them with his sunglasses.

He was sex. He was sin.

He was her worst nightmare.

He was her hottest fantasy.

He was standing in Stella's driveway!

She'd feared her crude stepcousin since she was seven and he'd cut off her waist-length hair with Stella's sewing scissors. She'd loathed him since that day when she was a very naive seventeen and he'd kissed her—seduced her—arousing womanly desire in her for the first time. Then, when she'd lost any will to resist, he'd set her aside with a caustic remark. He'd stalked from the room without a backward glance, leaving her half-naked, hot and humiliated. His cruelty had devastated her shaky confidence and made her careful of involvement with men, fearing the pain of other rejections.

She'd tried to forget that day, nearly had, in fact. But, Lord, he looked good . . . and dangerous.

"Wh-what are you doing here?" she asked, mortified at the croaking sound she emitted.

"I could ask you the same question, Princess," he said, insolence dripping from each word. "Did you come to kiss me goodbye?"

"Kiss?" She'd ice-skate in hell before doing that again. "Where are you going?"

Then she knew.

Wade Taggart intended to go with them!

Her mind reeling, she turned to Stella, struggling to keep panic from her voice. "Is *that* what you forgot to tell me?"

Stella's hands fluttered to her cheeks. "Oh, dear. It won't be a problem, will it?" She glanced from Laurel to Wade and back. "I guess I did forget."

"Yes, dear," Laurel said, barely able to keep frustration from her tone.

Wade frowned. "You bet your sweet—"

"Wade! Don't swear in front of Aunt Stella!"

"—*heart,* you did."

A slow, sexy grin played across his sensuous lips. Lips she remembered all too well. Lips she'd tried to forget for twelve years.

Blast the man!

Drawing into herself, Laurel raised the defenses against Wade Taggart she'd hoped never to need again. She forced herself to speak calmly. "Aunt Stella, you said we'd go and scatter Uncle Homer's ashes at places that were special to you." Tossing what she hoped was a dismissive glare at Wade, she added, "We don't need *him* or anyone else."

He's cruel and shiftless, she wanted to add, the *last* man they needed.

Three weeks in a car with Wade Taggart? Unthinkable.

Stella shrugged as if the matter was of no consequence. "Oh, but we do. Or I do. I need both of my darlings to be my guardian angels now that Homer is gone."

Laurel stole another look at Wade. *Guardian angel?* More like the devil himself, she thought, struggling to suppress the warmth coiling in her core. He was definitely Prince of Darkness material.

"Now that you're both here, let's get going." Hoisting her big purse, Stella marched toward the garage.

"But, Aunt Stella..." Laurel scurried after her, growing desperate. "We have everything planned for the *two* of us. Just tell Wade there's been a misunderstanding. You and I will go together on this wonderful adventure you've planned for us."

Without waiting for a response, she turned to Wade. "Why don't you just leave quietly? You're really not needed."

"Why, *Princess,* don't *you* leave quietly?" He mimicked her high-pitched tone.

She ground her teeth at that nickname. He'd called her that since childhood, his tone making the word an epithet. "Because I want to do this."

"Why so self-sacrificing, Princess?"

Because I love her, and I owe her. Stella and Homer had filled the role of grandparents to a child who had none. Their warm affection had given her a sense of acceptance, of being loved for herself alone. Laurel wanted to shout her frustration at the family's black sheep—a juvenile delinquent who'd grown up and, from all appearances, had become an adult delinquent.

"I bet you have something *really* important to do," he continued, "like visiting one of those health spas where a fleet of servants peels grapes for you."

"I *did* give up something important for this vacation with Aunt Stella," she fired back. "I'd planned to—"

She stopped herself. She'd intended to teach summer school because she could put the extra money toward the adult literacy center she planned to establish in her small town. But she would cut out her tongue with a butter knife before she'd let Wade know that for several years she'd lived modestly on her teacher's salary and saved systematically so she could help others.

He expected the Laurel he believed her to be: a rich, spoiled brat. That's what he'd get. Especially if she revolted him so much that he'd can the idea of going with her and Stella.

"I'd planned to attend the Summer Charity Ball," she lied airily, "then head for Antibes with Biff and Muffy... and Lud, of course."

She'd never been to Antibes and wasn't even sure it was still a favorite playground of the wealthy, but Wade certainly wouldn't know, either.

"Biff and Muffy and Lud? Do people really use names like that?" he asked, his tone a mix of disbelief and contempt.

No one she knew these days. "In the right circles." Arching an eyebrow, she scanned him with a cool gaze to indicate that he would never be a member of a "right circle."

Actually, she had never fit in with the socialites she'd grown up with. She'd been shy, awkward and far too serious for those superficial people. She much preferred her newer, down-to-earth friends among the school faculty.

"So this Lud, is he your latest boyfriend? With a name like that he'd have to have lots of money—old, moldy money."

"His name is Thomas Elliot Yeats," she improvised, plucking the names of three poets from the recesses of her memory.

"Well, Ms. Right Circles, this trip's too rough for you. You might break a nail, and we wouldn't want you to suffer a trauma like that." He flashed her his maddening grin.

"I have no intention of leaving Aunt Stella alone with the likes of you."

"I'm not bailing out, either, Princess." He shifted his focus to Stella and his tone gentled. "You said you needed my strength and common sense to protect you, and I want to do that for you. I promised Homer I'd look after you. I rearranged my schedule to spend this time with you."

"Had to pass up a meeting with your parole officer, I presume?" Laurel said, her tone satisfyingly contemptuous.

Wade bit back a curse. He'd built a successful business. His skills were in demand all over the world. By anyone else's standards he was a success.

But not Laurel Covington's.

With a few words and an imperial expression, she'd reduced him again to the thirteen-year-old ruffian so angered by her cold refusal to include him in her birthday party that he'd dumped an ice cream sundae on her party dress.

"You're amazing, Princess. Who'd believe someone six inches shorter could manage to look down her nose at me?"

"You haven't changed a bit, Wade."

Actually, only his appearance was the same. His comfortable old clothes, three-day beard, hair in need of a barber—probably even his classic, cosmetically impaired Lamborghini—were all the evidence Laurel needed to reach the wrong conclusions.

Over the years he'd wondered about her, wondered if she'd changed as much as he had. Well, the answer was a resounding no. His cousin was still the pampered, self-absorbed daughter of a rich man.

She wasn't really his kin, of course. Her father had emphasized that on more than one occasion. A niece of Homer's had had the poor judgment to marry Wade's father, to be his stepmother for a few years when he was a child. When she died, his only link to Laurel's blue-blooded family had been Stella and Homer.

To Laurel he was still the bastard at the family reunion.

He tamped down the urge to set her straight. To tell her he'd arrived home at dawn from New Zealand with jet lag, worn out from three months of working eighteen hour days. He'd wanted nothing more than a hot shower, a shave and a long night's sleep. But he'd promised Stella he'd be here, and he'd been running late. So he'd stuffed a few clothes into a duffel bag and jumped into his treasured car, hoping the tour-hour drive from Dallas would put the rebuilt engine through its paces and help him unwind.

But why waste an explanation on Laurel Covington? She thought he was worthless, so he'd live down to her expectations ... and keep her at a distance. That should be easy enough. She'd always brought out the worst in him.

"Aw, hell, Princess—" he protested her assault on his character.

"Don't curse!" she snapped. "You're still crude—"

"And you're still a snotty—"

A shrill whistle rent the air. He turned toward its source as Stella withdrew two fingers from the corners of her mouth. "Am I going to have to separate the two of you like I did whenever you both landed on my doorstep? Some guardian angels you are," she snorted, "acting like children in need of a lesson in manners!"

Wade curbed his temper, remembering that his purpose was to indulge Stella's wishes. After all, she and Homer had taken him in with a welcoming hug each time his itinerant father had dumped him without notice, each time he'd run away from some shack that served as a temporary home.

Placing a placating hand on her shoulder, he said, "Sorry, Stell. I didn't mean to upset you." Over her head he glared at Laurel, then realized most of the effect was filtered out by his mirrored sunglasses.

He'd do anything for Stella; he owed her more than he could repay in his lifetime. He'd even put up with Princess Laurel. He'd forget the way she'd been at seventeen, trembling in his arms, yet exploring his mouth with an erotic combination of innocence and sensuality. He'd forget how her silky, blond hair slipped through his fingers, how her pale, firm breasts filled his hands, how her sky blue eyes showed curiosity and fear. He'd forget the anger her needless fear engendered in him, taking her roughly until her soft body melded with his hard one, ardent and urgent—and forbidden.

Jeez! He turned his back and lifted the duffel bag from the passenger seat, then held it awkwardly in front of himself to conceal his body's miserable failure to forget Laurel Covington.

He made himself look at her again—at the real Laurel. Hair pulled up into a sleek knot, eyes of blue ice, lips drawn into a thin line. She was as she appeared—a spoiled society snob.

Forgetting who she was had nearly brought him to disaster twelve years ago. And could again.

With his free hand he scratched his belly, a gesture meant to disgust her. A slight curl of her lip signaled his success. He wished he could belch at will. Or that he could spill ice cream on her again.

"So, ladies, let's get this show on the road." He slung his duffel bag over his shoulder, strode up the driveway and opened the garage door. But he froze when he got a look at the rusting body of a tiny, yellow subcompact.

"Is *this* your car, Stell? Where's the nice, sturdy sedan Homer bought a couple of years ago?"

She smiled proudly. "I traded it in on this cute thing."

She was actually taking this wreck out on the roads? He didn't want to alarm her, but damn!

"They don't even make this car anymore," he said mildly. "Where will we get parts if it needs repairs?"

Stella glanced from him to the car and back, seeming confused by his question. "It doesn't need parts, dear. It runs just fine."

That heap hadn't run just fine when it came off the assembly line. They couldn't take off on a trip to God-knows-where in that pile of junk.

"How about taking your car, Princess?" he asked desperately. Surely she drove a big luxuro-cruiser, and possibly, he thought grimly, she'd condescend to permit a dirty bum like him to ride in it.

"I took a cab from the airport." From the look on her face, the princess was equally stunned, equally appalled.

"Wade, dear, you don't understand," Stella said, sounding like he had a case of the stupids. "It's part of the surprise. Don't you see—we'll travel like Homer and I did on our honeymoon fifty years ago! We could only afford an old, rusty car, sort of like this one. We'll pack sandwiches and eat at cheap cafés. I even bought these old clothes at a garage sale so I'd feel more like those good old days."

She must have read something into his expression, for she added, "And as I told you, I insist on paying for everything because you've both been so good to me. I can easily afford nicer things, but I think this way will be more fun."

With a knuckle, she scrubbed away a tear from the corner of her eye. "I want the three of us to have a lovely time."

She turned big, guileless eyes on him, and he melted. He'd hold that heap together with wire and willpower, if necessary, to make her happy.

"Of course it'll be fun," he managed to say. "We'll take your car. I'll just give it a quick once-over to get familiar with it, then we'll be on our way."

He noted the worn tires and sagging exhaust pipe, then raised the hood, not surprised to find oil splattered everywhere, worn belts and hoses and nearly empty fluid tanks. Stifling a curse, he closed the creaky hood and smiled stiffly.

"It'll be fine. Just fine," he lied. Good thing he had a wallet full of credit cards. He promised himself he'd replace the worn parts as unobtrusively—and quickly—as possible. "Shall we get started?"

While Laurel and Stella checked the house to be sure the doors and windows were locked, he jammed his duffel bag in the car trunk and parked the Lamborghini in the garage, his thoughts on his stepgreat-aunt.

She was growing old, he realized, and Homer's death had been hard on her. Yet in many ways she seemed as indomitable as when she'd pulled his youthful self up by his collar and talked to him about right and wrong—something no one else, except Homer, had ever bothered to do for him.

Without their encouragement, he'd never have gone to college, never have tried to make a better life for himself. Stella had always been proud of his accomplishments, even though she had no clear idea what he did for a living. After trying unsuccessfully to explain his consulting business, he'd simply told her he fixed business stuff and made a lot of money doing so. She thought he repaired office equipment, and she was delighted with his financial success.

Her request for his help with her mission had grabbed him around the heart. She'd been secretive about their destinations, but it didn't matter. He'd drive into hell and back if Stella wanted him to. For the first time in her life she needed him, and he'd be there for her, no matter what.

He'd even put up with Laurel Covington, the one woman he'd hoped never to see again.

Heat waves shimmered from the car's dented hood as Laurel watched Wade stuff an ice chest into the narrow space behind the front seat. In one arm she cradled the red-lacquered, Chinese-style urn with Homer's ashes, and she extended the other hand to Stella to assist her into the back seat.

"Wait," Stella said. "Pictures. I want to make an album of our adventures just like Homer and I did." She fished around in her purse and withdrew an ancient instant-print camera. "Stand here by the car, my dears, and smile."

Laurel dutifully stood where she was told, with three feet of space between her and Wade.

Holding the camera to her eye with one hand, Stella motioned with the other. "Closer. I can't get both of you in the picture."

Laurel took a grudging half step toward Wade, despite the urging of her instincts to put *more* distance between them.

"I said closer." She waited as they narrowed the gap again, then pressed the button. As the picture developed, she frowned in disappointment. "No smiles. Try again."

The second picture revealed Laurel and Wade smiling with the warmth and sincerity of a couple of sharks, Laurel thought on viewing it. Stella tucked the snapshot away without comment.

"Ready?" Laurel asked. At Stella's nod, Laurel helped her into the back seat.

"Give me the urn, dear."

"It's top-heavy, Aunt Stella. Uncle Homer's ashes will be much safer if I put the container on the floorboard and steady it with my feet."

Laurel crawled into the cramped passenger seat, settled the garish container, then anchored it with her feet. She had to be crazy, or at least as eccentric as Stella, to offer to ride around guarding her uncle's ashes like a penguin hatching its red lacquer egg.

Wade crowded into the driver's seat, the steering wheel mere inches from his chest, his shins pressed against the dash. His broad shoulders encroached into Laurel's space, forcing her to press against the door to avoid touching him. A hint of male sweat wafted in the sweltering air.

Sexy, her body proclaimed.

Disgusting, her brain corrected.

Three weeks of Wade Taggart. Dear God! What, she wondered, was a nice girl like her doing in a place like this with an urn between her feet?

"Are we ready?" Stella asked.

"Ready," Wade and Laurel chorused. He started the car and turned on the air conditioner.

"Well, then, get going, dear."

"Um, Stella, you're the only one who knows *where* we're going. That was part of your surprise," Wade reminded her.

Following Stella's directions, he drove through the streets of Austin and out onto a highway. The air conditioner fan whirred energetically, blowing hot air into the stifling car.

"Fiddle with the knobs, Princess. We need to cool off."

"How perceptive," she said sweetly, then tried in vain to coax cool air from the ancient equipment.

Wade drove to the far side of Lake Travis and stopped near an open, rocky area that passed for a beach in the Texas Hill Country.

As she helped Stella from the car, Laurel noticed several sunbathers lying near the water's edge, seemingly immune to the sun's searing rays.

"What a lovely place, Aunt Stell— Oh, my God!" She leapt between her aunt and a sun worshipper who'd stood up. "He's naked! Don't look!"

"Of course he's naked, dear," Stella said patiently. "This is Hippie Hollow. It's been a nude beach since the sixties."

"But, but—" Laurel sputtered, resolutely keeping her eyes downcast.

"Homer and I came here often until his health failed," Stella continued, waving cheerfully at the inhabitants. She snapped a picture.

Laurel choked trying to suppress a delighted laugh. Stella and Homer had gone naked in public!

"Cool, Stell," Wade said, a good-natured chuckle lacing his voice.

Of course it was cool, Laurel thought. A couple of senior citizens comfortable enough with their bodies to bare them in the presence of a group of twenty-somethings.

But the snobby princess that Wade presumed her to be would never find such "vulgarity" acceptable, so she schooled her face into a disapproving frown.

"Hey, you gawkin' geeks," a nude woman shouted, "get nekkid or get outta here."

"Okay." Wade started to pull his T-shirt over his head.

"Don't you dare!" Laurel warned from between clenched teeth. Keeping Wade at a distance would be hard enough when he was fully clothed. Naked— Her heart slammed against her chest at that vision.

"We don't have time to sunbathe today." Stella interrupted Laurel's errant thoughts. Taking the urn, she added, "Follow me."

She turned away from the beach and strolled into the woods. Fifteen minutes later she paused to study first the ground then the oak and mesquite trees, looked toward the lake, shook her head and walked on.

Puzzled by this odd amble, Laurel wondered what Wade thought. Steeling herself, she caught his eye with a silent question. He raised a shoulder in a half shrug, seeming as mystified as she was.

After repeating the search process several times, like a dog trying to find where he'd buried a bone, Stella nodded and handed the urn to Laurel. She lifted off the top, tipped the container and carefully poured ashes into her cupped hand. With a wan smile, she scattered the ashes over the ground, then closed the container and hefted it into her arms.

"Thank you, Homer dear, for the lovely memory," she said softly. After a moment the smile grew into a grin that brought new light into her eyes. She dragged the camera from her bag and handed it to Wade. "Take my picture."

Posed beside a tall oak tree, smiling for the camera, Stella looked lovely and content, Laurel thought. At ease with herself and coming to terms with the loss of her husband of more than fifty years. After a moment

Stella walked resolutely toward the car, chuckling to herself.

Stella and Homer had loved each other so freely and deeply for so long. Every woman dreamed of such a devoted, unconditional love. Few were as fortunate as Stella, Laurel acknowledged.

She had hoped for such love, but she'd failed to find it with Phil, and her marriage had ended amid treachery and abandonment.

Perhaps someday, someone . . .

Chapter Two

As Wade followed Stella to the car, he shook his head in bemusement. Stella and Homer had frolicked naked on a public beach when they were seventy years old. He admired their spunk, though he'd had a hard time containing his surprise. In fact, if Laurel hadn't been there, he'd have let his embarrassment show.

But the man she believed him to be wouldn't think twice about stripping in the presence of a crowd, so he'd pretended that public nudity was nothing unusual for him. He would be eternally grateful that Stella had called a halt to his striptease before he'd made a spectacle of himself.

In truth, he appreciated the human body most when he was alone with a special woman . . . and sunbathing was the last thing on their minds.

He looked at Laurel and thought he glimpsed regret in her eyes when she flicked a glance at him. Except for

being stuck with him for three weeks, what did she have
to be sorry about?

When they climbed back into the car again, the
temperature must have been over one-fifty. Waiting for
Stella's directions, he started the motor, and Laurel
turned on the air conditioner.

"Do you think it healed itself in the last half hour,
Princess?"

Looking very regal, she silently patted her glowing
face with a tissue. He wondered if she ever permitted
herself to break into a real sweat.

"Where to now, Stell?" he asked, unaccountably
irritated and wanting to get underway.

"Why, back home, dear."

"Home?" His voice rose an octave in disbelief.

"We just left home," Laurel said, masterfully stat-
ing the obvious.

"I'm tired and need a good night's sleep so I'll be
ready to go in the morning. But you two young people
won't have to stay with me. I want you to have fun this
evening."

Why had they packed the car? No, he wouldn't ask.
But all he really wanted was a long night's sleep. He'd
been awake for at least thirty-six hours, but his reck-
oning was uncertain because of multiple changes in
time zones, not to mention crossing the international
date line.

"What kind of fun?" Laurel sounded less enthusiastic than he felt.

"You should go to Sixth Street, of course," Stella
said. "That's where all the trendy clubs and bars are
these days. You can go dancing."

He'd rather be shot. "Uh, Stella—"

"Homer and I used to dance the night away, but I'm too old for that now."

"You're not too old to dance a little with me." If she'd go with them, perhaps he could avoid talking to the princess, or having to touch her.

"But I don't want to," she said tartly. "I want you young people to have a nice evening together before we leave. You'll be stuck with this old girl for three weeks. I don't want you to get bored."

"Sounds like fun, doesn't it, Princess?" he said with false enthusiasm.

"Oh, yes," she cooed while shunting him a look that said "Touch me and you die."

As he drove them to Stella's house, Wade considered his wardrobe problem. He'd brought along several pairs of casual slacks and a selection of knit shirts—clothes that a successful, thirtyish entrepreneur would wear. Clothes that his adopted persona— the one Laurel believed was the real Wade—would sneer at. The T-shirt, jeans and boots he wore, the only grubby garb he'd brought, would have to do.

Then there was his three-day-old beard. It itched like crazy, but he'd better keep it. He couldn't risk looking clean-cut.

An hour later, buoyed by two of the baloney sandwiches Stella had packed in the ice chest and by a long, cool shower, he joined Laurel in the living room. Her quick scan of his clothes and the wrinkling of her nose signaled his success.

"Relax, Princess. We're not going to the Governor's Ball. I washed my shirt and put on clean underwear," he said, keeping his tone laconic. "Did you?"

"Did I what?"

"Put on clean underwear."

"That's none of your business!" Her cheeks pinked prettily, he noted. Baiting her was almost too easy.

"Sure it is. If I wreck my Lamb—*car*—and you have to go to the hospital, I'd be real embarrassed if your underwear wasn't clean. Your whole family would be disgraced."

"*Your* car?" she asked in a strangled voice. "You expect me to ride in that—that blood clot on wheels?"

"It's part of the adventure, Princess. Ready to go?"

Stella clapped her hands together. "Oh, my! Homer and I had a little two-seater. We had such fun! The stars above us. The wind in our hair..."

"The bugs in our teeth," he muttered just loud enough for Laurel to hear.

He'd have sworn she flashed a smile for an instant before covering it with a frown.

"Oh, all right," she said grudgingly. She stood beside the car, waiting for him to open the door, and eyed with obvious distaste the primer coat, the cracked leather upholstery, and the rearview mirror held in place with masking tape. Her slender, sensuous body was draped in a wispy, blue floral jacket and wide-leg crepe trousers that swirled about her long legs.

"Your carriage awaits, Princess. Climb aboard."

She tugged open the creaking door and settled herself on the lumpy seat in a froth of soft fabric.

"Wait!" Stella barreled into the garage, waving the camera. "I need a picture of this." Taking careful aim, she snapped the picture, watched it develop, then dismissed them. "Have a lovely evening, my dears." With a broad wink, she added, "I won't wait up for you."

"Hang on," Wade ordered Laurel and fired up the engine. She placed a hand primly on the dash to steady herself against the sudden vibration. Accelerating faster than necessary, he shot the Lamborghini down the driveway. She sucked in a quick breath and grasped the dash with both hands, leaning against him as he swept into a sharp right turn.

Momentarily pleased with her discomfiture, he quickly realized he'd outsmarted himself. Only thin layers of fabric separated her soft, supple body from his. He reached for the gear shift, his hand brushing her leg. Lightning flashed up his arm. He heard her gasp again as she shifted her leg in the cramped space.

Her sudden movement pressed her hip against his. To distract himself, he counted backward by threes from a thousand until he reached their destination—a parking lot a couple of blocks from Sixth Street.

He leapt from the car and strode along the sidewalk in the gathering dark, fast enough that she had to hop-skip to keep up. Fast enough that he couldn't see her, touch her.

As they rounded a corner, loud, angry curses and shattering glass burst around them. Five men ran from an alley, heading their way. More footsteps pounded behind them.

Trouble.

Spotting the only available shelter, he grasped Laurel's arm, forced her into a narrow doorway and shoved her back against a rough wooden wall. Bracing his forearms on either side of her head, he leaned over her.

"What—" she gasped, her eyes wide with fear. Her hands pushed against his chest, seeking escape.

"Shut up and stand still!" he ordered in a rough whisper. "We're not part of their fight. Maybe they won't notice us."

Angry voices grew louder and more violent as others joined the melee. Rocks, bottles and fists found their targets. She said no more and stopped struggling, but he felt her trembling, heard her breathe in shallow gasps.

Wanting to protect her, wanting her to *know* he'd protect her, regardless of his opinion of her, he pressed against her from thighs to shoulders, sheltering her fragile body with his own. Her soft sigh, her sweet mouth, the scent of her hair, the very essence of her, nearly undid him.

He caught her gaze. Blue flames flared in her eyes.

Fear.

Desire.

He wanted to caress her, soothe her with whispered endearments. Kiss her again and never stop. But the sane portion of his brain reminded him of the surrounding violence—and that the woman in his arms needed only his momentary protection. Nothing more.

Teeth gritted, he closed his eyes and stood unyielding until the raucous crowd began to break up at the sound of police sirens.

Something hard and sharp slammed against the side of his head. "Sh—!"

"What happened?" Laurel asked in a panicky tone.

"Bottle hit me." He felt a warm, wet ooze on his scalp. He hoped it was beer, but the odor was wrong.

"Where?" she breathed.

"Head."

Her fingers combed gently through his hair, searching until she traced a laceration, making him wince.

"Good heavens, you're bleeding!"

"Sorry, Princess. I'll try not to get any on your clothes."

"My—my clothes? Oh, no. No." Her voice was shaky, and he wondered if she would faint at the sight of blood on her hand.

"Okay, buddy! Break it up!" A deep, harsh voice jolted him and he turned his head to face a beefy cop.

"Raise your hands and step away from the woman!"

I'm the good guy! he wanted to shout, but his addled brain wouldn't form the words.

Raising his night stick, the cop repeated his order and Wade managed to comply.

"You hurt, ma'am?" the cop asked solicitously.

"No," Laurel whispered from behind Wade. "I'm all right." Her voice gained strength. "He kept me from getting hurt. But he's got a cut on his head."

The cop looked dubiously from Laurel, the lady, to Wade, the bum. He must have noticed the oozing blood, for his harsh expression softened. "Do you feel dizzy? Should I call the paramedics?"

When he shook his head, the officer watched his eyes for a minute. Apparently satisfied that Wade wasn't a hazard to himself or anyone else, he said, "Better get that tended to. Head wounds are no joke." With that advice he strode down the street in search of the long-gone combatants.

Princess Laurel had spoken up for him! He felt pleased for a moment until he realized he was grateful to her for telling the simple truth. He'd better watch himself. Something about her turned his brains to mush.

"Princess, I think I've had all the Sixth Street fun I can stand tonight. Want to watch 'em stitch my head at a Doc-in-the-Box?"

Raising an imaginary camera to her eye, she said, "Smile, dear. I need a picture of this moment."

He had to be hallucinating. Surely the princess hadn't made a joke while his blood congealed unnoticed on her fingers.

Laurel squirmed, seeking a less uncomfortable position in the hard plastic chair as she pretended to read a tattered copy of *Healthy Living*.

Two empty seats away, Wade sat slumped forward, patiently waiting his turn. Fingers slowly massaging his forehead, eyes closed against the too-bright lights in the all-night clinic, trickles of blood crusting on his right temple, he could have been a medieval knight, exhausted from a day of dragon slaying.

Wade Taggart, a hero?

Stop it! He's just an overgrown delinquent.

But courageous, her mind nagged.

He'd surrounded her with his powerful body, swamped her senses with the scents of soap and man. She'd forgotten her fear of the street violence for a moment, caught up in the turbulence of her unwanted sexual response to him and her memories of the pain he'd once caused her.

She tried again to focus on Ten Tips for Healthy Toenails, but her brain refused. In the midst of a riot, when she was on the verge of panic, he'd thrust her out of danger. He'd turned his back to a maddened mob, shielded her without thinking of his own safety.

Get real, she ordered herself. Wade probably brawled in the streets for entertainment. Protecting women was just part of his macho image. It impressed some women, she guessed, but not her—at least not once she'd had a moment to think about it. She'd known what he was like since she was ten and he'd disrupted her birthday party, ruining one of the few special days she'd shared with her parents.

Her father had told her then that Wade was a thief. *He repaid Stella and Homer for their charity by stealing a bicycle and embarrassing them. He's as worthless as his old man.* He'd told her about juvenile delinquents and bad seeds and warned her to stay away from Wade Taggart.

Good advice. She should have followed it.

Wade hadn't changed much, except that he was even bigger, stronger and more virile than he'd been at twenty, when he'd kissed her, roughly at first, as if he were capturing an enemy, then gently exploring her mouth and body, awakening a woman's responses in her. Then he'd shoved her away with an insult.

Blast him for being . . . well . . . him. And blast the emotional storm—the attraction/aversion—that raged within her at the mere sight of him.

"Mr. Taggart?" A nurse, petite and pretty, smiled warmly as she emerged from the curtained cubicle. "The doctor will be with you in a few minutes. If you'll step over to my desk, we'll clean you up a little while we wait for him."

Her gaze scanned him from scalp to boots as he approached, her smile growing warmer and wider. "Now, what happened to you?" she cooed—in a thoroughly unprofessional manner, Laurel thought.

"I disarmed a guy by smashing my head against his broken bottle," he said with "aw-gosh, ma'am" modesty. "Figured I'd need a few stitches."

The woman continued to fawn over him as she pulled on surgical gloves, sponged away dried blood and inspected the gash that began at his right temple then disappeared into his thick, dark hair. That done, she led him into the cubicle.

Laurel pretended to engross herself in the article on toenail maintenance while eavesdropping as the doctor sutured Wade's wound and told him how to care for it and when to have the stitches removed. A few minutes later he emerged sporting a large, cushiony bandage. The nurse accepted his cash payment and handed him a plastic bag of supplies and another one full of crushed ice. "Are you sure it's safe for you to drive? I could call a cab."

Wade assured her he was mentally and physically sound, and the nurse continued, "Just hold that ice against the wound for an hour or so to prevent more swelling, Wade. Do that right away, now."

Laurel swore the woman batted her eyelashes at him. *The flirt.*

"Yes, ma'am." Wade flashed her a million-watt smile, his teeth brilliant white against his beard-stubbled face.

The hound.

Outside, he stepped into his car without a word until she'd seated herself.

"Here, Princess. Hold this on my head while I drive." He plopped the ice bag into her hand, then started the engine.

Irritated by the nurse, by Wade, by her outrageous hormones, she flopped the frigid sack against his temple. His startled "Ow!" gratified her beyond words.

On the seemingly endless trip to Stella's, she clutched the dash with one hand and pressed the ice bag against his head with the other. Her breast brushed his hard, corded bicep. She gritted her teeth against the sparks that raced through her and carefully avoided touching him intimately again.

She didn't care who flirted with him—or who he flirted with, she told herself.

So he was sexy. She'd known that since she'd reached puberty.

He was dangerous. She'd known that since she was ten.

He was cruel. She'd learned that at seventeen, when she was innocent and vulnerable.

She would not put herself at risk again. She only had to keep up her princess act and remain withdrawn and distant.

As withdrawn and distant as possible, while she struggled against overeager hormones and ministered to Wade's combat wound while they raced through the hot, dark night.

"Dear boy, how is your injury?" Stella danced on tiptoe the next morning, stretching to examine Wade's wound.

"It'll be fine when the aspirin kicks in." He bent at the knees until his head was level with hers so she could inspect the bandage.

"Well, let me know if the aspirin doesn't work. I've got a whole pharmacy in this purse—ibuprofen, acetaminophen, Chinese herbs—you name it."

"Thanks, Stell, but I'm okay." In truth he felt like someone pounded a bass drum inside his skull while marching over his brain in heavy boots. For an instant he was sorry he'd insisted on making this trip. A day with an ice pack on his head in a cool, dark room was an appealing fantasy. But he'd promised, and after last night he was even more convinced that he was essential to Stella's safety—and Laurel's.

So he would ease his pain with aspirin, drive that cramped junk heap and try to ignore the oppressive heat—and Laurel.

"You're looking none the worse for the wear," he observed to his nemesis, letting his gaze rove slowly over her face, slightly pinkened in the early morning heat. She wore a fashionable tan camp shirt and walking shorts. She looked elegant, despite the temperature and humidity that left him sweaty and irritable.

"Well, Stell," he said to divert his thoughts, "everything's ready, so let's take a picture and hit the road." Standing beside Laurel in front of the car, he forced a smile and waited for the click of the camera.

That accomplished, he helped Stella into the back seat, then wedged himself behind the steering wheel. Laurel settled in beside him, sandaled feet cuddling the urn, hugging her door as though it were a life preserver.

After several tries, he got the car started. "Where are we going today, Stell?"

"Dallas!" she crowed.

It figured. He lived in Dallas. They could have met him there, and he'd have been spared a slashed scalp and a world-class headache.

Out on the highway he brought the car to its cruising speed—a whopping forty-five miles per hour.

"Try the air-conditioning again," he told Laurel, hoping against all reason that it would work more efficiently than it had in yesterday's stop-and-go traffic.

Her dark glare asked whether he thought the car had "healed" overnight, but she fiddled with the knobs. He thought she muttered something, but he couldn't hear her above the rush of sweltering wind pouring through the open windows.

"You have your choice of temperatures," she announced finally with a frustrated sigh. "Steaming, boiling, blistering or scalding."

"I'd prefer torrid...smoldering...sultry," he drawled, flicking her a sidelong glance to see if she'd picked up on his sensuous word choices.

"You would." Her lips drew into a tight line.

"I'm doing fine back here," Stella volunteered.

And she was. Wearing purple-framed, heart-shaped sunglasses, she rested her back on a pillow she'd wedged against the side of the car, her short legs propped on the seat. She'd attached a battery-powered fan to the open lid of the ice chest and relaxed in the relative comfort of a thin stream of cool air.

She dug around in her huge purse, finally pulling out a package of particularly noxious cigarettes. She snagged a lighter and soon was puffing away.

"Aunt Stella!" Sounding scandalized, Laurel turned to face her aunt. "You're smoking!"

"Yes, dear," she said in that too-patient tone. "Mind Homer's ashes."

"But you don't smoke. You always said it was a dirty habit."

"Well, of course it is. But I smoked like a barbecue pit on our honeymoon, even though Homer didn't like it much."

"But it's bad for you," Laurel persisted.

"I didn't know that then, dear. But I haven't been in a coma for the last forty years. I know smoking is bad for my health."

She released another voluminous puff. "So I won't inhale. I'll just pretend to smoke for old times' sake." She opened a magazine and began flipping the pages.

Wade bent to Laurel and muttered in her ear, "It could be worse. If we had air-conditioning, we'd have to breathe secondhand smoke for the next three weeks."

"Lucky us," she murmured. "*Clean* torrid, smoldering, sultry air." A smile played at the corner of her lips and her eyes lighted. "Tell me if my hair catches on fire."

He flicked her a grin and a wink.

Her smile vanished, and she squeezed herself against the door again, staring at the featureless highway as if it were endlessly fascinating.

"Excuse me, Princess. For a moment I thought you'd turned human."

She continued to inspect the highway in silence.

At mid-morning, Stella made peanut butter and grape jelly sandwiches and passed one to each of them, along with cans of off-brand cola. Wade ate the sticky-sweet mess, struggling manfully not to gag as a large lump of it stuck to the roof of his mouth.

"PBJ sandwiches were the mainstay of our honeymoon meals," Stella volunteered. "We couldn't afford cafés all the time, so we made do."

Laurel nibbled daintily at her sandwich, but a big purple glob slid between the crusts and dropped onto her lap. She dabbed frantically at the mess with a tissue, then with a chunk of ice from the cooler, but she managed only to spread the goo into a bigger circle on the front of her walking shorts.

He sighed elaborately. "I can dress you up, but I can't take you out, Princess."

"This," she said in a tone as sweet as the jelly, "from a man who thinks dressing up means washing his T-shirt once a week, whether it needs it or not.

"Oh, good heavens!" Laurel said before he could set her straight. "There's a police car behind us. Its lights are flashing! Pull over, Wade."

"Aw, hell, Princess. Sure you don't want to outrun him?"

As he slowed the car and pulled onto the shoulder, she frowned. "Are the police looking for you?"

Blast the woman. She had no reason to think he was guilty of anything. "No. I haven't committed any crimes lately. And thank you very much for the vote of confidence."

"I just wondered why a policeman would stop us. We certainly weren't speeding."

As the car ground to a halt, Stella lit another cigarette, filling the passenger compartment with smoke.

The officer walked to the car and looked inside. "Driver's license and insurance certificate, sir."

Wade pulled out his license. His yuppie self stared at him from beneath the laminate. Lord, he missed being that comfortable, well-rested man.

"This picture doesn't look like you, sir."

Stella piped up helpfully, "That's because Wade just got back into the country, and he's had a beer bottle smashed on his head. You'd look awful, too, if it'd happened to you. And, Wade, dear, do you need some stronger drugs?"

She hauled her huge purse into her lap and began fishing for her drug supply.

"Hold it!" the officer said. "Hand me that bag, ma'am. Then everybody keep both hands in sight at all times."

Stella handed over the purse with shaking hands and a stricken expression. The officer dug through grocery receipts, snapshots, handkerchiefs, maps and cigarettes and pulled out her supply of over-the-counter remedies. He handed back the purse with a frown.

"Is the insurance receipt in the glove box, Stell?" Wade asked, hoping to soothe Stella's nerves with a mundane question. He popped it open only to find it empty.

Stella choked on smoke, coughing and gasping for several moments. "It's at home, I guess," she wheezed. "Homer always took care of the paperwork, you know."

"I'll have to give you a ticket, Mr. Taggart. The reason I stopped you is to let you know your left rear wheel is wobbly. Could be dangerous."

"Officer, smile please," Stella instructed, holding the camera to one heart-framed eye. In a moment she added a picture of a startled highway patrolman to her collection.

Wade accepted the ticket and thanked the officer for his concern.

"Excuse me, miss," the officer interrupted, his gaze on the floorboard, "but I'll have to take a look at that container between your feet," he said with polite firmness, pointing at the urn.

"But they're my great-uncle's ashes," Laurel said defensively, her face flushing like she'd been caught smuggling crack.

"Hand it to me *now*," he said, still marginally polite.

She grabbed the urn with one hand, opened the door with the other and leapt outside.

"Freeze!"

The officer stood like a rock, aiming his revolver at Laurel's chest.

Jeez! Did the princess have a death wish? And what in the world could he do to help her?

"But they're *ashes,*" she repeated, raising her hands, one clutching the garish urn, in surrender.

"Oh, Homer, dear Homer!" Stella wailed.

"Put the container on top of the car and back away real slow, lady. *Now.*"

Laurel complied, eyes wider than a doe's in headlights.

"Wade!" Stella grabbed his shoulder. "Don't let that man throw away Homer's ashes! He'd *hate* it if this ugly highway was his final resting place."

"Uh, officer," Wade said, working at sounding like he regularly chatted with gun-wielding cops about bizarre topics, "I'd appreciate it if you'd be careful with your examination. Those really are this lady's husband's ashes. We're scattering them at some special places."

He started to ask rhetorically if he looked like a drug runner, then concluded that he probably did, with his old clothes, scraggly beard and sweat-crusted head bandage. But he had the two unlikeliest accomplices and the worst getaway car on record.

The officer took a long look at him, at Laurel, trembling visibly, and at Stella, near tears. Holstering his gun, he carefully lifted the top off the urn, looked inside, then closed it.

"Everything seems in order." He returned the urn to Wade. "Proceed, but have that wheel looked at." He returned to his patrol car, massaging the back of his neck with one hand.

Laurel reclaimed the urn, planted it on the floorboard and gripped it with her feet, then sagged against the seat.

She looked frightened, vulnerable. In need of a comforting hug. But not from him.

"Now you've done it, sweetheart," he drawled, trying to sound like Dogey. "Your mug shot's gonna be in cop shops across the country under the heading, Ash Dealer. Won't surprise me none if they stop us again, maybe strip search us, now that they've got a line on you and this swell car. Me and the old lady's got to ditch you to save ourselves. Sorry, sweetheart, but that's the way it is when you cross the line into a life of crime."

"Stuff it, Wade," Laurel snapped, eyes flashing. Then she collapsed, crossing her forearms on the dashboard and resting her head on them. Great, heaving sounds tore from deep in her chest. Bursts of laughter, he realized after an agonized moment.

"Dammit, you're *awful*," she gasped. "Truly awful."

"Mind your swearing in front of the old lady, sweetheart."

Chapter Three

A few miles later, when Laurel thought she might expire from the lethal combination of heat exhaustion, the shock of being on the wrong end of a policeman's gun and prolonged exposure to Wade Taggart, he pulled in at a truck stop.

Spotting a mechanic, Stella waved and called, "Yoohoo, sonny, I need a nice used tire."

"Why don't you ladies go inside where it's cool, and I'll handle the tire," Wade said firmly as he assisted Stella from the back seat.

Bracing herself against the car, Laurel stood on one leg, lifted the other and rotated her ankle to relieve the urn-induced cramp, then repeated with the other ankle. Stella snapped a picture of her. Swell, she thought. She'd be immortalized on film posed as a flamingo.

She followed Stella to the blissfully cool ladies' room. The older woman promptly lit a cigarette. Smoke grew thick in the small, poorly ventilated room, and Laurel feared she'd gag as they took turns splashing tap water on their faces and necks to rinse away the top layers of dried sweat and highway grime. Despite the effort Laurel felt sticky and less than half-clean.

She considered working on the purple stain on her shorts, using the slimy pink hand soap that dripped from a grubby plastic container above the counter. Then she remembered she had a suitcase full of clean clothes.

Stella followed her outside, saying, "I'll see if I can help that sweet boy. Isn't he wonderful? Aren't you glad he was along to handle that policeman for us? And the tire business?"

"Oh, yes," Laurel said with barely concealed sarcasm. Then she realized she *was* glad Wade was along. Despite their animosity, he'd spoken calmly to the highway patrolman and defused a scary scene after she'd panicked, thinking for a crazy moment that Wade really was wanted, and jumped from the car to protect Homer's ashes.

He'd teased her, too, breaking the tension that had constricted her chest so she could hardly breathe.

Wade Taggart could be charming when he wanted to. She pushed that thought away. Thank goodness he rarely turned his charm on her, or she'd be in real trouble.

"I'm so proud of Wade," Stella said, her eyes alight. "He's made such a success of himself, with that business of his. Why, he travels all over the world, you know."

Yeah, right. Wade an international traveler—maybe to stay ahead of the police.

She must have looked dubious, for Stella added, "He sends me picture postcards from everywhere he goes—London, Rome, Paris, and most recently from Auckland, New Zealand. His life is so exciting!''

Why in the world would Wade go to the trouble of finding foreign postcards just to mislead his sweet great-aunt? Why pose as something he wasn't? Stella would always love him, no matter that he was in his thirties and hadn't amounted to much.

She shook her head, bemused. Just when she'd nearly convinced herself that he had some redeeming qualities.

"Um, Aunt Stella, does he ever ask you for money?"

"Why, no, dear." Her brow furrowed as if the question made no sense. "He sends me lovely things, though. I'm sure he can easily afford them."

Oh, sure. Lots of prosperous businessmen owned one faded shirt and one pair of shabby jeans and traveled in a rolling junk heap.

"Come along, Laurel, let's see if we can help him." She strolled into the blazing heat and headed for the young mechanic who was working under the hood of her car.

Wade, cradling the scarlet urn in one arm, intercepted her and herded her back inside. "Stay where it's cool, Stell."

"All right, dear," she agreed, wiping fresh perspiration from her forehead. She snapped a picture of Wade looking fairly ridiculous himself. "You seem to have everything under control."

As she returned indoors, he muttered to Laurel, "Keep her inside where she can't see what's going on."

"What are you up to that she shouldn't see?" she asked warily.

"Nothing nasty, Princess. I'm having the wheel replaced, getting five new tires and having the oil changed and several belts replaced. Oh, yeah, and a shot of coolant for the air conditioner."

"Why can't she know?" Laurel chided herself for extending the conversation. She needed to get clean clothes from her suitcase, and she didn't want him watching her dig through her personal items.

He'd taken off his sunglasses, she noticed as he caught her gaze, then lowered his thick, dark lashes in a lazy, sensuous blink that caught her off guard. His eyes weren't black, as she'd always believed. Nor were they cold. In the afternoon sun, gold flecks danced in the irises.

"Why ruin her fantasy that traveling in a worn out car is romantic?" he asked.

Intrigued with his warm gaze, she was barely aware that he'd spoken.

"Earth to Princess? Do you read me?" His mouth tilted into a knowing half smile.

Drat! He'd caught her staring at him, lips parted like a teenager with a crush.

"I take it you're an expert on romance?" she said sourly.

"I haven't had any complaints, Princess. How about you?"

Only one. And the memory still plagued her, especially when the complainant stood before her. "Forget it, Princess," he'd said, as he pushed away from her after seducing her body and soul. "You aren't woman enough for me. Never will be."

He'd savaged her fragile self-confidence with those words, and with the way he'd wiped the back of his hand across his mouth as if the taste of her repelled him.

Now Wade's half smile made her wonder if he remembered that night. Probably not, she decided. Drawn by the promise of sensual thrills in his darkly dangerous sexuality, impressionable females likely threw themselves at him with such frequency that they became indistinguishable to him.

She hoped so. She hoped she wasn't the only fool.

"We need to locate your insurance agent or the company and get a copy of your coverage, Stell. Otherwise we'll have to pay a hefty fine and risk getting more tickets," Wade said twenty minutes later. He blinked as Stella took a picture of him with the receiver in hand.

"Now, there's no Robert Redford listed in Austin under insurance agents," he added.

Laurel suppressed a smile as he dropped another quarter into the pay phone. She felt a little better now that her clothes were clean, even if she wasn't.

"Let's try again to come up with the name of the company," he continued kindly, showing no sign of frustration even though he'd already made a half dozen calls to directory assistance and to wrong numbers.

Stella rubbed her forehead with her thin fingers, obviously tiring. "They all sound alike, you know," she complained. "American Union National Statewide General Liberty Something Something."

"I'll try General Liberty this time." Several calls later, he reported that there was such a company, but it never had a policy for Homer or Stella Martin.

Sitting beside Stella on a scarred wooden bench, he took her hand in both of his. "Let's get something to eat, then we'll try again."

"Good idea," she said crossly. "I don't like to do business on an empty stomach."

Clearly, Stella did not like doing business under any circumstances. Laurel thought again how interdependent her great-aunt and uncle had been. But as a result, Stella was unprepared to handle "paperwork," because Homer, an efficient businessman, had taken care of such things for them. But he'd failed to teach Stella how to manage on her own.

When the vacation was over, Laurel promised herself, she'd sit down with Stella and organize her finances, making sure everything was paid up. Then she'd teach her aunt to handle matters on her own so she could maintain her independence and her dignity.

Stella led them to the grimy lunch counter that looked as though it was on the Department of Health's hit list. They sat on stools covered with faded green plastic that had been frequently mended with gray duct tape. Stella captured the grill and cook with her camera. Without consulting anyone, she ordered barbecue platters for three.

Laurel groaned inwardly as her meal was served from pans of greasy, gray meat covered with bright red sauce, gelatinous creamed corn and limp green beans.

"Homer always loved good barbecue. It's filling and cheap at places like this," Stella observed, aiming the camera at her plate.

While Stella ate with gusto, Laurel managed to down a couple of bites of what was *not* good barbecue, then rearranged the food with her fork, pretending to eat.

Beneath lowered lashes, she watched Wade carefully avoid his meal, as well.

As Stella wiped her lips, he said, "Let's try again to get in touch with your agent, Stell."

"I think it's Paul Newman," she said as she slid off the stool and headed for the pay phone.

Walking behind Stella, Wade rolled his eyes and muttered to Laurel, "When we finish with Hollywood, we can try the NFL."

Nevertheless, as Stella stood at his elbow, he tried Mr. Newman's name on directory assistance, followed by three other possible company names and John Wayne, to no avail.

Grudgingly, Laurel silently thanked him for his patience and persistence. He, too, seemed to respect their great-aunt's dignity. But why had he told her such ridiculous lies about his job?

Stella snapped her fingers. "Of course! It's Mel Gibson!"

Wade flashed Laurel a here-we-go-again grin and dialed.

Thirty minutes later agent Melvin Gibson had faxed two copies of Stella's policy to the truck stop. Laurel mailed one of the copies along with the ticket to the Department of Public Safety, relieved to have the problem of the fine resolved.

The mechanic presented Stella with a bill for one used tire, which she paid while complimenting him for the very reasonable price. And she took his picture.

Slanting a glance at Wade, Laurel saw him slip a credit card to the man. Who, she wondered, issued credit cards to people like him, people with no visible means of support?

Perhaps the Texas prison system had its own credit union.

"Now, my dears, aren't we having fun?" Stella chirped from the back seat as Wade cranked up the engine and headed for Dallas.

If this is fun, he thought, *hell must be hilarious.*

"Try the air conditioner again, Princess," he said, rubbing his throbbing forehead and yearning for a chilly breeze.

"Let's hope the mechanic healed it," she muttered, adjusting the urn between her feet, and turned the knobs. After a few minutes, the blast of hot air cooled down—about two degrees.

Damn! The coolant must have leaked out as fast as the mechanic injected it. He watched Laurel fiddle with the knobs, trying vainly to coax cool air from the wheezing equipment.

She'd rewound her blond hair into a tidier topknot, but a few escaped tendrils brushed her face and neck. He wondered again how she managed to look so coolly appealing despite the withering heat.

Unfazed, Stella set up her battery-powered fan on the ice chest lid and donned her outlandish sunglasses. "Wake me up when we get to Dallas," she instructed. In moments she was snoring gently.

Laurel smiled at him, a tentative curve of her luscious lips. "I appreciate your tenacity, Wade. I'm not sure I'd have had the persistence to ferret out Aunt Stella's insurance agent. You, um, surprised me."

"Surprised you, Princess? Because I stuck with something for thirty minutes?" he asked, forcing a light tone. What right did she have to be surprised about anything he did? She didn't know him; she just had opinions.

Her eyebrows drew together and her lips tightened. "I just meant—"

"That it's amazing that Wade Taggart can accomplish anything? Remember, Princess, I had to struggle for everything I got. As a kid I had to fight every schoolyard bully who figured he could take that scrawny, dirty newcomer. That was the only way I could prove—on a crude, elemental level—I was as good as anyone else. Later, I had to overcome a bad education just to get in, and stay in, college. I worked my butt off."

She gasped softly, her blue eyes darkening with pity. He hated that look. He'd seen it most of his life, worked tirelessly so that he'd never have to endure pity again. Why had he been so frank with Laurel Covington, of all people?

"Forget it, Princess," he said harshly. "You wouldn't understand. You never had to struggle for anything in your life. Everything you wanted was laid out for you. Still is."

He saw her press her fingers against her lips, close her eyes for a moment, then turn to study the highway. For once, she had nothing to say. Good, he thought, anger heating his blood. But he couldn't decide whether he was angrier with her or himself.

The uneasy silence lasted until dusk, when Stella woke up just outside Dallas. "Wade, dear, I meant to ask if we can stay at your lovely high-rise condominium tonight? Homer and I often stayed with friends and relatives to save money, even though that wasn't much fun on a honeymoon."

Laurel rolled her eyes, then frowned at him, apparently convinced that he lived in a refrigerator crate in an alley.

He should have expected Stella's request. And he'd like to save her the cost of motel rooms. But he lived in an upper-middle-class neighborhood with all the trappings of a successful businessman—two-hundred-bottle wine cellar, atrium, hot tub and too many bathrooms.

If Laurel had a look at the place, he'd blow his cover. The ne'er-do-well he was pretending to be would never get past the security gate, much less be able to afford the mortgage payments.

"Gee, Stell, I wish I could invite you, but I, um, there's not enough room," he improvised desperately.

"Just spacious enough for you and the cockroaches?" Laurel asked.

"Perfect!" Stella enthused. "Most of our friends were as poor as we were. Homer and I contended with roaches, fleas and sometimes bedbugs!"

"Aunt Stella," Laurel interjected firmly, "I really think we need to stay at a motel, preferably one without vermin."

"Oh, all right," Stella agreed with a pout and a muttered comment that sounded like "no fun at all."

Wade's feeling of relief lasted until Stella said, "Stop right there," and pointed to a dilapidated brown building with a sagging roof and a blue neon sign that read E ZY MO EL.

Refusing to second-guess his decision, he escorted Stella to the office to pay for the rooms. They located their quarters at the end of the bleak row, and Wade lugged the baggage to their adjoining rooms.

"Don't take time to unpack now," Stella said. "I'm hungry."

A quick inspection of his room confirmed that the sheets were clean, if frayed. The shower not only worked, it sprayed hot water. For Stella's comfort, he hoped the room she and Laurel shared met at least this bare minimum.

And there was no need to worry about roaches. The odor of insecticide permeated the air. He could picture the princess wrinkling her nose at the first whiff.

He called his office, half hoping that something had come up that required his immediate, undivided attention—or at least would take his mind off the princess. Marla Thompson, who'd worked with him since his lean and hungry days, assured him that everything was under control, and he gave her instructions for handling several items that needed attention.

"So how's the trip with your great-aunt?" Marla asked. "Earned your Good Samaritan badge yet?"

"You wouldn't believe how messed up this quest is. First, she forgot to mention that her rich, obnoxious grand-niece was coming along. That woman drives me crazy with her fancy airs and her nasty temper. Then I got my head busted open trying to rescue her."

"You're hurt?" Marla's concern was refreshing. Good old Marla, the only woman in his life he could count on, except for Stella.

"Not bad. It's just irritating."

"So, what does this cousin, or whatever, look like?"

"Lots of long, blond hair piled on top of her head, a haughty, I'm-too-good-for-you expression."

"Gorgeous, huh?" Marla teased.

"No, a princess."

"Sure, boss." She clearly didn't believe him.

"Look, content yourself with being my ace secretary and leave my personal life alone," he said with more heat than he'd intended.

"Or you'll fire me again," she taunted with typical disrespect.

"One of these days, I'll really mean it," he grumbled. "I'll call you as often as I can. Say a prayer that something comes up that only I, the Great Wadeini, can fix."

"Want to dump the sweet old lady, you heartless beast?"

"No. I just need to think about something besides my miserable state." He hung up and joined the women.

After Stella treated them to an indigestible meal at the tacky diner across the pothole ridden parking lot, and she'd taken a couple of pictures, she lit a cigarette and announced, "Tonight I want you two to enjoy yourselves."

"Enjoy ourselves?" he asked incredulously. "How?" To him *enjoyment* meant downing more aspirin, taking a long, hot shower, changing his bandage and collapsing into bed. But with a sinking feeling, he realized Stella had something else in mind.

"By going dancing, of course. Last night your lovely evening was cut short by that nasty accident, so you'll have to make up for it now."

He turned to Laurel, hoping she'd come up with an excuse.

"I'm really tired, Aunt Stella—"

"Nonsense. You're too young to be tired. Now get dressed up and go."

"I'd really rather rest," Laurel persisted.

"But...but you *have* to go," she fretted, twisting her hands. "Homer and I loved to dance. I *need* for you to go dancing like we used to. You'll have fun!"

He thought she would burst into tears. As he led them across the parking lot to the "MO EL," he searched for a way out that wouldn't hurt her feelings. Every cell in his body longed for a hot shower. But if he satisfied that craving, he'd fall asleep before he managed to dress for the "fun" evening.

I love Stell. I'll do anything to make her happy. Repeating those statements in his mind as though they were a mantra, he accepted the inevitable.

"Ready, Princess?" he asked.

Her shoulders sagged, and she let out a long breath that would have been a sigh if Stella hadn't been there.

"Sure. Why not?"

"Good." Stella regained her good humor and fished in her purse. Aiming the camera at them, she commanded, "Now smile."

Laurel sketched a smile and a wave at Stella that matched his own and climbed into the car beside him.

As he drove along the freeway, Wade wished he could take her to his favorite continental restaurant. The tuxedoed staff would greet him deferentially by name, despite his grubby appearance, and the food and service would be impeccable. He'd surely impress her. He rejected that idea. He didn't want to impress the princess—probably couldn't, at any rate. She'd always taken for granted the finer things in life.

Instead, he watched for the right kind of bar. Sol's Place fit his needs, he decided, as he turned into the parking lot; it advertised "DANCING FOOD".

"I'd like to see that," Laurel ventured.

"What?"

"Dancing food. I wonder if various dishes perform different routines."

He laughed in spite of himself. "Perhaps it just isn't dead yet."

"Lovely thought. Fortunately I'm not hungry. After today I may never be hungry again."

His stomach rumbled in empathy as he opened the door to Sol's. It had been years since he'd been in a joint like this: smoky, grimy, smelling of stale beer and staler cigarettes. Neon beer signs glowed in the near dark, eerily illuminating men and women of all ages who wore jeans and cowboy hats. An amateurish country-western band struggled painfully to capture a hit tune, the volume precluding all but the most urgent conversation.

Definitely a dump. Perfect for his adopted persona.

A waitress wearing tight jeans, a skimpy halter top and too many pounds took their orders. He started to request his usual, an English ale, but caught himself and settled for a cheap domestic beer.

"Can I see the wine list?" Laurel asked as though she were in a four-star restaurant.

"We got beer, honey. Regular or light. What'll it be?"

"Whatever he's having." Her nose wrinkled when she said *he's*, he noted. They both declined an opportunity to sample the food, destined never to know whether the fajitas could do the Texas two-step.

He watched Laurel scan the scenery through the smoky haze.

"You like this place?" he shouted above the din, knowing it was stranger than a third-world country to her.

Laurel shrugged, picked up the less-than-sparkling glass the waitress set down beside her beer and eyed it in the gloom, then set it aside. She wiped the top of the bottle with a paper napkin and took a sip.

He watched her pale throat work as she swallowed. She managed to look elegant, like royalty with the common touch, as she sat in a dive and sipped cheap beer. He took a pull from his longneck, then studied the crowd instead of her. She looked too good.

A tall, lean, tough-looking man strode toward their table, giving Laurel an unhurried once-over as he approached. He tipped the brim of his hat up with the curve of an index finger, then held out his hand, palm up. "Care to polish my belt buckle, pretty lady?"

She hesitated, then caught Wade's gaze, holding it for a second before turning back to the man.

"I—"

"No, she wouldn't. She's with me," Wade objected, shocked at his vehemence.

"I'm here under duress," she said, and flashed Wade an angry look. "However, I am not 'with you.' This is not a date."

She stood, took the cowboy wannabe's hand and gave him a sweet smile. "Thank you. I'd love to dance with you."

Wade ground his teeth as the interloper put his hand at the small of her back, guiding her through the crowd to the dance floor. The man held her so close she had to be miserable in his clutches, Wade thought with satisfaction.

Then the man turned her slowly, and he saw her tilt back her head and laugh, looking more relaxed and happy than she'd been in the past two days.

Dammit. He was jealous of a loser in a third-rate bar. Because Laurel smiled at him, let him take her in his arms and dance. Wade wanted to be that man. Wanted to have no history with her.

Wanted to be able to hold her without risking rejection or ruin.

When the song was finally over, she shook her head in response to something her partner said. He shrugged, then led her back to the booth.

"Thank ya, honey," he said. "You're a real good dancer." With a tip of his hat, he turned and headed to the bar.

"I think I've seen enough to give Stella a convincing account of a fun night on the town," she said when the man was out of earshot.

"Sure you don't want to dance with the rest of the drunks?"

Ignoring his outburst, she squared her shoulders and marched out the door.

He followed her across the parking lot. "You've got no sense, Princess," he said to her retreating back, loud enough that several people craned their necks to check him out.

"The guy looked dangerous," he persisted, although common sense told him to shut up. "Unshaven, wearing grubby clothes, beer on his breath."

"He looked like you, with a cowboy hat," she snapped. "And smelled better. Besides, *you* didn't ask me to dance."

"I'm just trying to look out for you."

"You don't own me, Wade. You don't decide who I dance with."

"Well, hell. Come on. Get in the car."

She raised her chin and glared. "I will, but only because *I* want to. Not because you told me to!" She flung open the door.

Onlookers applauded and whistled. "Tell him, lady!" "Don't take no crap off him, honey!"

She settled herself like Queen Elizabeth in her royal coach and closed the door. He half expected her to wave regally to her faithful subjects.

He got in beside her and slammed the door so hard the car shuddered. He drove to the motel, cursing under his breath.

Finally, *blissfully,* rid of Laurel for the night, Wade took more aspirin, then reveled in a shower for thirty seconds until the hot water supply was exhausted. He practiced his vocabulary of curse words again.

He changed the bandage on his head, recalling the nurse's sure touch as she'd applied antiseptic cream. He wished for a human touch now—Laurel's gentle fingers stroking his head, caring for him.

Fat chance.

Laurel's comments about his cleanliness—or lack thereof—came back with a sting. Tired though he was, he pulled a knit shirt and pleated cotton pants from his duffel bag and put them on. Dirty clothes in hand, he sneaked from his room like a thief. He considered going home to do his laundry, perhaps even sleep in his own bed. But he couldn't let himself get too comfortable. So he drove until he found an all-night Laundromat.

He managed to hold thoughts of the evening's events at bay until his T-shirt and jeans were spinning hypnotically in the dryer. Then he wondered how he'd gotten into such a stupid situation. He knew the an-

swer. Stella. This crazy trip meant the world to her. For
Stella he'd endure the hot, cramped car, bad food,
cheap motels ...

And outrageous encounters with Laurel Covington.
He let himself really think about her, something he'd
held off doing for two days. She was as devoted to
Stella as he was. But she'd earned her nickname, for
she was still haughty, rich and every inch a princess.

He'd taken perverse pleasure in his deliberate rudeness, in insisting she ride with him in the Lamborghini, in taunting her. She'd deserved every bit of it, he
assured himself.

He'd expected her to be cold, distant and conde-
scending. But she'd taunted him back with spirit. She'd
even revealed sparks of humor. He wondered why she
always suppressed them so quickly.

All in all, he had to admit, she'd been a good sport
about the oppressive heat, the nude beach, the awful
meals, the picture-taking, the ash bust. Sometimes—
for a few consecutive minutes—he actually liked her!
That was more dangerous than wanting her.

And want her, he did. She'd made him lose his hard-
won self-control at the drop of a hat—a cowboy hat,
at that. She'd stood nose-to-nose with him in the
parking lot, eyes flashing as she asserted her independence.

Fire and ice.

She was as beautiful as ever—maybe more so now as
a mature woman. He recalled the feel of her supple,
sensuous body pressed against him in the doorway near
Sixth Street.

Remembering that, he hadn't dared ask her to dance
with him tonight. He knew he couldn't casually hold

her in his arms without wanting to explore her body again with his hands and mouth.

He'd seen fear in her eyes last night during the ruckus. But he'd seen desire, too. He'd wanted to protect her and possess her with the same intensity as twelve years ago.

At that time he'd been twenty, working his way through college and not sure he'd make it. Uncertain that he could break the cycle of poverty and passivity that had dogged his family for generations.

He'd known all too well that Frederick Covington would go to any lengths to keep his precious daughter away from the likes of Wade Taggart. Despite his urgent desires, his heated body, Wade had realized if he made love to Laurel that night, he could have her only once. Then her father, their circumstances and her attitudes would put an end to it. He'd decided he'd be better off not knowing what loving her was like.

And he'd always wondered.

He hadn't been good enough for Laurel Covington then, and he never would be, no matter what he made of himself. He'd never have the right family tree, the prestigious diplomas, the impressive club memberships. None of those things should matter in the nineties, but in the Covington family they were all that mattered. Witness her marriage to her father's partner, and her dating that Lud guy she'd wanted to go to Antibes with.

He'd been a fool to fall in love with her then.

He'd be insane to let it happen again.

He deserved a special page in Stella's photo album under the caption Disaster Waiting to Happen.

Chapter Four

"I'm glad we got an early start, Aunt Stella." Laurel surveyed the cloudless morning sky from beneath the brim of her straw hat and dabbed at her sweat-dampened forehead as they entered Fair Park in the heart of Dallas. She stifled a yawn, the vestiges of a restless night.

"We'll have another scorcher today, dear, but we must press on." Stella opened her ruffled pink parasol and held it at a jaunty angle over her head. "Now, I must find the right place." She led Laurel and Wade past the carnival rides, deserted until the Texas State Fair began in October. She paused to photograph a small lagoon where more paper cups than water lilies floated amongst the algae. Moving ahead, she halted every few minutes, turning her head slowly from side to side to gain her bearings.

Wade toted the flashy urn in the crook of his arm but said nothing. He'd said very little, in fact, while they'd eaten indigestible breakfasts and driven to the park. Fine, Laurel thought, careful to keep at least four feet of space between them. She had nothing to say to him, either.

She'd made a fool of herself last night in that low-rent bar. If she'd been celebrating a win with her faculty bowling team, she'd have had a beer or two, joked around and danced with her buddies. But she couldn't afford to let her hair down and try to enjoy the evening with Wade. So she'd done her princess number and asked for the wine list. When the cowboy asked her to dance, she'd accepted. She hadn't particularly wanted to dance with him, but Wade's attitude pushed her into it. Then she'd finished off the evening by screaming at him in the parking lot.

At that moment she'd wanted to make Wade jealous, of all stupid things. She'd wanted *him* to hold her in his arms, wanted to polish *his* belt buckle, not some stranger's. Her spine tingled at the thought of splaying her fingers against Wade's chest, their bodies swaying together to a slow ballad. Sheer idiocy. Did she thrive on rejection? Wasn't one round with Wade and another with Phil enough?

"This is what I love about living in Dallas in the summer," muttered the object of her wayward thoughts. "Ninety degrees by nine o'clock, the air filled with ozone and pollution." He raised his mirrored sunglasses and squirted drops into his bloodshot eyes, then offered her the small plastic bottle.

"Late nights will irritate one's eyes worse than the environment," she said primly, waving dismissively at the bottle.

"Spying on me, Princess?" he asked lazily.

Uh-oh! She dabbed at her warm cheeks with a tissue, hoping he'd think the heat rising there came from an external source. After he'd brought her back to the motel, she'd heard his door open and close. Eventually, perhaps hours later—she hadn't been able to read her watch in the dark—he returned to his room. No doubt he had a girlfriend, or a bevy of them, stashed in Dallas. Maybe he lived with one of them.

A wave of jealousy swept through her at the idea of Wade making love to a woman. Ridiculous. She had no claim on him. Didn't want to have anything to do with him. He could have sex with anyone he chose. It didn't matter to her.

Liar, taunted a little voice in her mind.

"The walls were paper-thin. I couldn't help but hear you leave," she managed to reply, pleased at the sneer in her voice.

"Yeah, Princess, I know. I couldn't help but hear you taking a shower." That damnable grin spread across his lips, a mocking smile.

Forcing an erotic vision from her mind, she walked quickly to Stella's upwind side to avoid a cloud of cigarette smoke. "Are we getting close?"

Her aunt stopped to study the art deco structures and twirled her parasol absently. "I'm not sure. They've changed some things since we were here."

"When were you and Homer here?" Laurel asked, to focus her attention away from Wade.

"Why, we met here just after the war. Homer was still in the army, and he was on leave. I was a can-can dancer in the floor show at the fair." She shrugged eloquently. "Well, you know...."

Wade's chuckle was deep and warm behind them. "I always thought you had a secret past, Stell. Showed a bit of leg on the stage, did you?"

"More than a bit, dear."

Laurel laughed, then quickly bit her lips to silence herself and adopt a starchy expression. She wondered if her staid parents had any idea that they'd left their daughter in the care of a "wild woman."

"Give us a show, Stell."

"Well . . ." She glanced around and, apparently satisfied that she wouldn't draw a crowd, set down her bag and handed Wade her parasol. Singing "tah-rah-rah-*boom*-dee-ay," she lifted imaginary skirts and kicked her slacks-clad legs in a passable can-can.

Delighted with her aunt's spirit, Laurel grabbed the camera and took her picture. She couldn't resist taking one of Wade, looking like he belonged in a police lineup, but cuddling the red urn in one arm and holding aloft the pink parasol with the other.

Breathless, Stella stopped and subsided on a wooden bench. "Not bad for an old broad."

"You were great," Laurel said. "But don't wear yourself out in this heat."

Stella sat for a few minutes, breathing deeply and eyeing the scenery. "There!" She pointed to a narrow gap between two buildings. She pulled off her sunglasses and ambled up and down the dank passageway, paused and sprinkled ashes, then asked to have her picture taken.

Laurel frowned, worried about Stella's disorientation. Why in the world would this dark, grimy place remind her of a special occasion? She glanced at Wade to gauge his reaction. He lifted a shoulder, looking mystified.

"Ladies, we'd better get moving before we fry our brains."

As he led them to the parking lot, Laurel watched his loose-hipped stride and lectured herself silently about risk taking. True, Wade was kind and gentle with Stella, but he lied to her about his world travels. He could be funny, charming even. But he also was sarcastic, arrogant and rude.

His outburst about having to fight bullies as a kid and struggle to get through college had touched her. Now she wondered how much of that was true. Perhaps he'd just enjoyed fighting and had drifted through college as he was drifting through life.

He wasn't much different from the eighteen-year-old who'd spent the summer glowering at her, refusing to speak to her without prompting from Stella or Homer. At fifteen, she'd been lonely, an outsider at a new school. She'd looked forward to spending time with her uncle and aunt, surrounded by their comforting love.

But within a week Wade had shown up, clearly disappointed to find her there. He'd watched her as though she were something he wanted to scrape off his boot heel. She'd tried to make conversation about school, sports and movies, but he'd answered in grunts, if he answered at all.

He'd rejected her even then. If she'd been more perceptive, she could have avoided disaster two years later.

"Ouch!" Laurel massaged her upper arm where Wade bumped her with his shoulder.

"Princess," he growled, "it's my job to drive the car, which means I have to be able to steer it. Which means your job is to stay out of my way!" He bit back curses directed at her, himself, his bandaged head, the blasted

car, the heat and finally the entire universe—except for
Stella, the true cause of all his miseries.

A glance in the rearview mirror assured him she was
as comfortable as possible. A contented smile lit up her
face and soothed his jagged nerves.

"Where to, Stell?"

"Amarillo, dear."

Amarillo? A four-hundred-mile trek? He had to be
nuts to have agreed to travel with Stella—and the princess—without knowing where they were headed, what
he was getting into. He always counseled his clients to
get all the facts and analyze them carefully before
agreeing to any proposal. He should have taken his
own sage advice.

"Have you got a highway map, Stella?" When she
retrieved one, he added, "Take a look at it, Princess.
You might as well make yourself useful and navigate."

Laurel unfolded and studied it for several minutes
and sighed. "We need to head north on Interstate 35,
then connect with Highway 287."

"Oh, no, dear, that's not the way Homer and I went.
We liked the byways. Give me the map."

Wade swallowed a groan. The trip would take a good
twelve hours at best. He knew enough about the road
system to realize that no single "byway" paralleled the
main highway. So they'd have to zig-zag on narrow,
winding roads for a day and a half before they reached
their next destination.

Pushing his lips into a semblance of a grin for his
aunt's sake, he said, "Great idea, Stell. We'll get to see
the countryside."

He didn't mention that in drought-stricken north-
west Texas the scenery would consist of mile after mile

of dead grass, tumbleweeds and scrawny mesquite trees. On second thought, Stella would probably be reminded of how much fun she and Homer had that time they nearly died of thirst.

Stella gave him directions. Then she busied herself with the contents of the ice chest and handed cans of cola and sandwiches to Wade and Laurel. "Tuna fish today," she said proudly.

Can't be worse than peanut butter and jelly, he assured himself. One bite of the cheap, oily tuna laden with mayonnaise and he realized he was wrong. Lord, what he endured for the love of Stell. He cut a glance at Laurel, who'd closed her eyes and held the malodorous sandwich at arm's length while she chewed.

"Careful, Princess," he muttered, "we don't want a repeat of yesterday's bad manners. Remember, tuna smells worse than jelly, so keep it off your lap."

Still chewing, Laurel shot him a fierce look. He thought for a minute she would shove her sandwich in his face. But no, the princess would never lower herself to his level. Instead, she surreptitiously dropped the remains of her sandwich out of the car window while Stella studied the map. Great idea, he thought, likewise disposing of his own lunch. He wondered if the buzzards could stomach the stuff.

Laurel pulled a sheaf of papers and a pen from a large envelope that the urn had been resting on. Leaning against the passenger door, she began writing, pausing from time to time to stare into space as if searching for inspiration, then returned to her efforts.

"Making an invitation list for your next party, Princess? Bet my name's at the top."

"I have a list where you're tops, but it's not for a party." Her tone could refrigerate the tropics.

He couldn't resist goading her again. "So, what are you doing? Preparing a report to the Manners Police about my activities?"

Her jaws clenched, and she spoke through her teeth. "If you must know, I'm making lesson plans. I'm . . . I work at a school."

"Miss Prim's School for Terminally Snooty Princesses?"

"Edgarville Public School."

"Edgarville? Down by Corpus Christi?" He remembered that small, impoverished town with dilapidated buildings and few good jobs. He'd lived there once for a few months until his father bought him a bus ticket for Austin where he'd stayed with Stella and Homer. Eventually his old man had collected him again and they'd moved on.

"Yes. I do hope you don't mind that I failed to ask your permission."

The princess in Edgarville? Then he figured it out. "You're with some do-gooder club for bored rich ladies," he accused. He remembered a few of those volunteers prancing around the classrooms. Overdressed and bejeweled, some showing pity, others showing blank faces. None of them had touched the unkempt kids, or tried very hard to help them. Princess would fit right in.

"So what do you do? Warn the youngsters not to eat their breakfast egg with a silver spoon 'lest it tarnish'?" He recalled one of those matrons solemnly passing on that advice to a roomful of eight-year-olds whose breakfasts of cereal and milk were provided by the school—never eggs, let alone eaten with silver.

Her laser beam gaze would have melted steel. "I teach first grade." She bit off each syllable. "And I am *not* a do-gooder."

She was gainfully employed? He didn't know what to say. Princess Laurel, who could have bought the whole town if she'd had any use for it, was teaching disadvantaged first graders. Why was she spending time at a hard job, working with kids whose lives were similar to his own grim childhood?

"Well, well, Saint Laurel's doing penance for—" *For what?*

"And she was voted teacher of the year!" Stella piped up from the back seat. "Weren't you, dear?"

"Yes," she muttered. Grasping her pen in a death grip, she began writing again.

Damn. He'd jumped to wrong conclusions, and he'd made her angry. He wanted to tell her he was sorry, he'd only meant to tease her. But the man she believed him to be would never apologize for mere rudeness. He had to keep up his deception for his own protection, so he said nothing.

And cursed himself.

The next morning Stella pawed through the long rack of cheap clothing and held up her prize, beaming proudly. "Perfect!"

"Oh, Aunt Stella, I can't possibly wear that skimpy outfit." Laurel nearly blushed at the thought of donning the thin, scoop-necked top Stella held up for her perusal. Not in public. Not with a huge pair of red sequin lips on the front. She glanced desperately down the aisle of juniors' sportswear the discount store offered. Surely there were clothes more suitable for a staid schoolteacher.

Apparently not.

"It's perfect for you. The color matches your eyes."

"My eyes aren't—" *Electric blue,* she finished silently.

"And I like this one, too." Stella shook a hanger for emphasis, and the iridescent colors shimmered in the harsh light.

When Laurel had opened her suitcase last night and discovered most of her clothes missing, Stella claimed she'd put them into the laundry chute at the motel in Dallas and forgotten them. Near tears, her aunt apologized and insisted on buying her a new wardrobe.

Struggling to mask her concern over Stella's mental confusion, Laurel quickly decided not to mention that the one-story motel had no laundry chute, no laundry room even. She'd bid a reluctant farewell to the fashionably classic wardrobe she'd assembled from resale shops.

She shook her head. Her aunt had preposterous ideas about fashion.

"Girls?" Stella called to two teenagers who were browsing through the racks.

"Yeah?" one of them responded around a wad of gum the size of a golf ball.

"Aren't these outfits terrific?"

"For you?" Gummy's eyebrows shot upward.

"Don't be silly. They're too young for me. I meant my niece, here."

The other girl, wearing unlaced combat boots and a tiny purple dress, eyed Laurel like a side of beef. Obviously uninterested in arguing with an old lady, she shrugged. "Way cool."

"Well, dear, these young ladies and I like these outfits."

"No," Laurel protested. "Not cool. No way."

"Way," Stella persisted, obviously getting into the swing of things.

Deciding on a different tack, Laurel said, "You don't have to buy me clothes, Aunt Stella. It's enough that you're paying for this lovely trip. I'll buy my own things." *And choose them, as well.*

"Nonsense, dear. This is my treat." She held up several more garments, as Gummy and Boots nodded approval.

When Stella snapped their pictures, they quickly backed away without another word and continued their browsing.

"Now, go try on these outfits."

Laurel made a tactical retreat to marshal her opposition. She took the pile of clothes to the tiny dressing room, donned an outfit and sighed at the image in the mirror. The fake leather skirt barely covered the essentials. She'd burn her bottom on the plastic car upholstery if she wore it. The tiny top revealed vast expanses of midriff and upper chest. Unthinkable.

Next she pulled on the tight-fitting top with sequins and tugged it down as far as it would go. Sure enough, the garish red lips snuggled in the valley between her breasts. Embarrassed at the sight of herself, she shed the garment and tried on the next . . . and the next. The other clothes made the first outfit look dowdy by comparison. Bright colors, stretchy fabrics, tacky styles. No, she couldn't possibly wear them.

Especially around Wade. Good Lord, with his ego he'd think she'd chosen this stuff to try to turn him on—and nothing could be farther from the truth.

She put on her own serviceable, beige dress and picked up the glad rags, prepared to firmly reject them. Surely she could make Stella understand.

"But, Laurel, dear," Stella objected on hearing the decision, "these are the clothes a young woman like you should wear when she's having fun and adventures."

So, when the heck do the fun and adventures start? "But—"

"No *buts,* dear. They're perfect for you. Besides, you should wear cute clothes if you want to attract a sexy man like Wade."

"Wade? I don't want to attract *Wade.*"

Stella's smile surpassed Mona Lisa's for being enigmatic. "Well, Wade wouldn't look twice at a woman who wears all that beige." She snorted her disgust with that color. "You're twenty-nine, dear, and there's no man in your life. Do you think your lesson plans will keep you warm at night?"

Helen Gurley Brown had taken over Stella's body!

"Aunt Stella, you know I don't...like Wade. You've seen how badly he treats me, and he always did. Remember when I was seven and he cut off my waist-length hair with your pinking shears? I had a bald spot on the top of my head." She rubbed that place, recalling the humiliation, compounded by her mother's lecture about letting nasty boys do such insulting things to her. As if she'd had a choice.

"Of course I remember," Stella said, her tone as soothing as when she'd comforted the young Laurel. "That wasn't very nice. But do you remember that only a week before, his daddy dumped him on my door-step? That boy was ten years old, motherless and had only the clothes on his back. Then you showed up, between private school and summer camp, and he was face-to-face with a girl who had every material thing a child could want, and two stable parents, to boot.''

"I...I had no idea..." Laurel closed her eyes against the guilt that washed over her. No, she hadn't realized that Wade's childhood had been so bleak. Even if she had, at the age of seven she hadn't been capable of understanding the frustration, the anxieties that abject poverty caused children. It wasn't until she began teaching, until she'd looked into the anguished eyes of her young students, that she'd begun to understand. She'd committed herself to help by teaching them to read, giving them an essential tool to lift themselves out of poverty.

"Now, dear, do these clothes fit you?" Stella asked briskly.

"Well, they fit, but they're not right for me," she said, setting aside her new insight into Wade's background.

"Wade will love them. Trust me on this, dear."

Was her great-aunt trying to fix her up? Aunt Stella was as determined as a terrier with a bone when she made up her mind about something. But surely even Stella wouldn't try matchmaking by outfitting her in trashy clothes and embellishing stories about "poor little misunderstood Wade."

"They're perfect. And you need clothes. You can't wear that old beige thing every day."

Drat! Her resolve was melting beneath Stella's pleas.

"All right." Stella sighed, "I'll wait until we get to Amarillo. There are fancier stores there. I'll buy clothes more to your liking." She had the look of a young child who'd been unjustly punished.

Laurel considered accepting the halfhearted offer. But department store clothes would cost a lot more, perhaps more than Stella could readily afford. She didn't know much about her aunt's finances, and she didn't want to be extravagant, to put her to needless expense. Muffling a weary sigh, she capitulated. She would wash her one decent dress almost every night, dry it with her hair dryer and wear it as often as she could without hurting Stella's feelings. The depth of her devotion to her aunt astounded her.

"No. You're right. They're perfect."

If she were playing a teenage hooker in a low-budget horror flick.

"What town are we heading for now, Stell?" Wade asked, wondering if they'd ever get to Amarillo. He grimaced at his image in the rearview mirror while Stella studied the map. He'd decided to forego the bandage since his wound seemed to be healing—the only positive development on this trip, he groused.

The doctor had shaved a band of his hair on either side of the wound, leaving him with a sutured gash in the middle of a bald stripe. His geek-of-the-week haircut was the least of his worries. The stitches itched, but not nearly as badly as his five-day-old beard. He wondered if he would ever get used to it. Would it stop itching, or was he destined to keep scratching for the rest of the trip?

While Stella and Laurel had gone shopping, he'd bought a beard trimmer to maintain the scruffy look that only terrorists or "Miami Vice" rejects would want to emulate. But that wouldn't do much for the itching.

The local thrift store had yielded several pairs of badly worn jeans and T-shirts. At least he wouldn't have to spend every evening washing the only disreputable clothes he'd brought with him.

Then he'd slipped off and called Marla to see if all was well in his real life. Unfortunately, no major disaster had popped up to provide him the opportunity to escape.

Stella pondered the map. "We just follow the signs to Seymour and then...we'll have to wind around a bit until we get to Crowell."

He started the car and brought it up to full cruising speed, and they crawled through the simmering heat at forty miles per hour, the dirt-laden wind sandblasting his face.

Laurel sat beside him, her body tensed as she leaned against the car door. She glanced his way, a troubled look in her darkened eyes, and for a moment he thought she'd speak. She must have thought better of it, for she steadied the urn between her feet, then bent her head over her papers and began writing.

"Wade, dear, Laurel's told us all about her career. Now it's your turn. I keep forgetting just what it is that you do, something about business things and computers. You fix stuff, don't you?"

For an instant he wanted to say, "I fix sick companies," to try to impress the princess with his accomplishments. Brag about his contacts and contracts, the places he'd been, the things he'd seen. The money he'd made.

Who was he kidding? She'd been all over the world, had enough money to buy several small countries.

"I get around, you might say. Move from place to place." From airport to hotel to conference room, then back to airport.... Getting around was wearing him down.

"Do you have a steady job?" Laurel asked, her tone and the arch of her eyebrows communicating disbelief.

"Me? What would I want with a steady job?" He'd tried that for a few years, then launched his consulting business, working from contract to contract.

"Oh, regular income, benefits, a chance to advance."

"That's fine for a dedicated public servant like you, Princess. But not for me. I'm footloose and fancy-free."

"And unemployed?"

"At the moment. That's why I had time to take this swell vacation with you."

"But, dear, you've been *everywhere*," Stella interjected, her pride in him written on her face. "I have the postcards to prove it. I look at them all the time."

Who'd have figured she'd kept the cards? "Yeah, I travel some. Mostly in the United States, though." That was true, too. He spent more time in major American cities than abroad.

"And Canada. I have that lovely sterling silver teapot you sent me from Vancouver."

"Silver plate from a pawn shop?" Laurel asked softly, her words lost in the wind before reaching Stella's ears.

Lord, she irritated him. He wanted to tell her what he'd paid for that eighteenth-century engraved pot at an antique gallery. Then he remembered his mission to live down to her expectations.

"Sure, why not?" he muttered. "She's easy to fool."

And so are you, Princess.

Chapter Five

Wade had finally changed his clothes, Laurel noticed at breakfast. Not that his sleeveless, faded T-shirt was much improvement. She read the four letters emblazoned across his amazing chest.

"Yale?"

"Yeah." He dropped a lazy wink, closing a lid over a gilt-flecked eye. "We make great locks."

"Locks? Oh." She bit back a snide comment, unwilling to start the day with a verbal fracas, and made herself focus on something more productive than staring at Wade's arms and chest. She consulted the guide book she'd picked up in the coffee shop. Amarillo offered a cattle auction, an aviation museum and a quarter horse heritage center, all unlikely candidates for "special places." What would Stella have in store today?

A couple of hours later, they were puttering along Interstate 40 in the slow lane, approaching Amarillo.

They passed by the downtown area and through the outskirts without a word from Stella. Laurel wondered if her aunt had gotten confused again.

"There! Over there, Wade!" Stella waved her cigaretted hand excitedly, nearly setting fire to Wade's hair in the process.

Across the highway Laurel saw what appeared to be a series of monoliths in a bare field. What in the world?

Wade, oblivious to his near hair loss, executed a series of turns and stopped on the service road.

"Cadillac Ranch," Stella said, her tone reverent. Clambering from the back seat, she commanded Laurel to bring the urn, unfurled her parasol and led them through a gap in the barb wire fence. Down a path in the pale brown grass, they neared a series of cars half-buried nose first in the parched earth.

Balancing the urn in the crook of her arm, Laurel flipped a page in the guidebook and began reading aloud. "Commissioned by local millionaire Stanley Marsh the Third—"

"Three," Stella corrected. "Stanley Marsh Three."

"Three," Laurel continued dubiously, "in 1969, a group of California artists—"

"Ably assisted by *Texas* artisans, including Homer and me," Stella interjected.

Laurel raised an eyebrow. "You and Homer were involved in this, um, project?"

"Yep, we helped select ten Cadillacs of various vintages, then upended them and buried their hoods in the soil of the Texas High Plains."

Laurel chuckled. She'd always known Stella and Homer marched to a different drummer, but helping to build this bizarre work of art—or kitsch—stretched her imagination.

"There's graffiti all over them," Stella said with a mournful sigh. "Kind of ruins the effect."

Right.

"Now, you two, stand by the second car from the right." When Laurel and Wade complied, she steadied the parasol's handle in one arm, raised the camera in front of her sunglasses and snapped a couple of pictures.

"Ready to go, Stell?" Wade asked, sweat dripping from his face.

"Of course not, dear." She handed him the parasol, squatted beside the car and crawled in through the windowless passenger door. Sitting on the ground inside the car, she lowered her head for a moment as if meditating, then caught Laurel's eye. "Urn."

Lifting the top, she removed a handful of ashes and pressed them carefully into the ground. She closed her eyes and smiled like a contented angel.

Pleased that this visit brought back such sweet memories to Stella, Laurel envied the joys her great-aunt and -uncle had shared for so many years. She'd dreamed of finding a man like Homer had been—gentle, hardworking, willing to share his home with a lonely grandniece and a delinquent boy who wasn't even a blood relative. He'd also had a sense of fun and adventure. And he'd loved Stella without reservation for fifty years.

Blinking back the tears that prickled her eyes, she thought of her probable future—alone, curled up with her lesson plans on long, lonely nights. *Enough self-pity,* she warned, abandoning her melancholy thoughts. Her knees weak from the noontime heat, she worried about her aunt sitting in that metal box.

"Aunt Stella," she said gently, "it's awfully hot in there. Perhaps you should come out now."

"In a minute, dear." She lifted dirty fingers to her lips, kissed them, then pressed them to the ground. "Thank you, Homer."

She crawled out of the car and reached for Laurel's proffered hand. "Oh...oh." Her hands fluttered weakly, then grasped Laurel's dress as she tried to stand. Stumbling, she fell to her knees, accompanied by a tearing noise as the front of Laurel's dress ripped open.

Before she could think, Wade stooped beside Stella and supported her shoulders, sheltering her from the sun with his body, and fanned her with his bush hat.

"Stell? Stell? Are you okay?" His voice was calm, but worry tightened his features. "Come on, love, we'll get you to the car and find a cool spot to rest."

With that assurance, he lifted her into his arms and strode to the road. Laurel gathered the urn, parasol and Stella's heavyweight handbag. Struggling to hold her shredded dress together, she hurried to catch up, her heart pounding with fear for Stella's well-being.

Wade started the car and pulled onto the road. The overheated interior cooled down to merely unbearable. Grateful for this small relief, Laurel twisted in her seat to keep a worried eye on her aunt. *Please be all right.*

"I'm all right, dear," Stella said as though she'd read Laurel's mind. "Don't trouble yourself about me. My knees ache a little, but that's all that's wrong with me."

In minutes Wade located a motel and carried a mildly protesting Stella to her air-conditioned room and laid her on the bed.

"I'll fill the ice bucket so you'll have cold water to drink, Stell."

"One of those colas would taste good," she hinted.

"I'll get the ice chest, as well. Laurel, you help her off with her clothes and cover her with a sheet." He turned to Stella. "We don't want you to catch a chill," he added in a voice gruff with emotion.

Surprised at his tone, Laurel recalled his attentiveness to their aunt. He did love Stella, she knew, perhaps as much as she herself did. She'd assumed that he was incapable of caring deeply. With only his treatment of her as a guide, what else could she think?

When he left, Laurel relaxed her fingers from their death grip on the ripped edges of her dress front. Before she did anything else, she'd change clothes. Then she remembered that her wardrobe consisted of outfits Stella had selected. The remains of her last decent outfit hung forlornly from her shoulders. She snagged four safety pins from her purse and pinned the front of her dress together to free up both her hands—and to conceal herself from Wade's eyes.

As she was helping Stella remove her slacks, Laurel's heart sank at the sight of the older woman's scraped and bloody knees. "We need to take you to a doctor. You've hurt yourself."

Stella considered her injuries. "Nonsense, dear. There's a first-aid kit in my bag. That'll do nicely for these scratches."

Laurel dragged a plastic freezer bag bulging with an assortment of first-aid supplies from Stella's purse. She was wiping her aunt's knees with an antiseptic towelette when Wade returned and saw the wounds.

"It looks worse than it really is," Stella maintained stoutly, but she winced when the antiseptic touched a particularly raw spot.

A muscle ticked in his jaw, but he said nothing as he filled a plastic glass with ice and cola and handed it to her with a tight smile as Laurel applied aloe vera gel and big gauze bandages to her aunt's knees.

"You don't look so good, either, Laurel." His dark eyes reflected concern. He filled another glass and handed it to her. "Drink up. The sugar should boost your energy."

If she hadn't known better, she'd have believed there was tenderness in his tone, in the way he looked after her. Sitting on the side of the bed, she took a sip of the too-sweet cola, then drank it down. Wanting more, she moved to stand.

"Here." Wade took the glass and filled it with more cola and ice. "Now, you ladies lie down and rest until I get back with our very late lunches."

He pressed his fingertips against the caps of Laurel's shoulders until her back lay against the pillow. "Take care," he said softly.

Definitely tender.

"Isn't he wonderful, dear?" Stella asked as the door closed behind him. "I feel so safe with him around. He handled my little mishap like a hero."

"Yes, he did," she agreed. This time her compliment was sincere. Wade had acted quickly to get them out of the heat, had given Stella gentle care. He'd been solicitous of her own needs, as well. Gentle. He'd even forgotten himself and called her Laurel, she thought wryly, wondering if he realized he'd mislaid his contemptuous attitude.

"Now do you see why you need to attract Wade with your nice new clothes? He's a lovely man." Stella rose from the bed. "I'm going to take a bath before lunch." With a spring in her step, she headed to the bathroom, humming softly.

Her aunt was amazingly resilient, Laurel thought. Despite injuries that appeared painful, she fussed over her niece's lack of a man in her life. Laurel considered her aunt's quick recovery. Surely Stella hadn't fallen deliberately to ruin Laurel's last decent dress or to showcase Wade's cool head in an emergency.

Surely not.

From the bathroom Stella cheerfully hummed a vaguely familiar old tune.

"It's So Nice To Have a Man around the House."

Laurel had just finished a quick shower and donned her favorite old bathrobe, covering herself from head to toe in faded blue cotton, when Wade returned carrying cartons of Chinese food and two bottles of thirst quencher. He gave her a long look and a mocking whistle.

"Wow, Princess, you've set a new standard for the word *dowdy*. Be still my heart." He turned his gaze to Stella's pink satin gown and gave her an elaborate wink. "Now there's a woman who knows how to dress."

Laurel ground her teeth in frustration. She was "Princess" again—and subject to Wade's insults. He had an amazing ability to tick her off every time she gave him the benefit of the doubt.

He dropped a quick kiss on his aunt's forehead and asked softly, "How's it going, Stell? I'll take you to a doctor if you don't feel well."

"I'm one hundred percent, dear," she said firmly, then favored him with an angelic smile. "I'm hungry, though."

Laurel served their meal on paper plates, then sat beside the grimy window in an uncomfortable chair, the partner to the one Wade had claimed. She ate hungrily, using the plastic fork rather than struggle with chopsticks for the sake of efficient consumption.

"Chinese food and bright blue thirst quencher—my idea of haute cuisine," she said between bites. Wade set aside the chopsticks he used as though they were his regular utensils and shot her a dark-eyed glare. "But," she added quickly, "I'll go into cholesterol withdrawal if you keep feeding me healthy food."

Visibly relaxing, he grinned, parted lips revealing even teeth, gleaming white in contrast to his tanned, bearded face. "Just part of Taggart's traveling companion services, ma'am," he drawled. "Always glad to have a satisfied customer."

She could get used to being cared for. Even if the care consisted of providing her with Moo Goo Gai Pan, no-name colas and brine-flavored thirst quencher in a third-rate motel room. Even if the care was primarily for her aunt.

Before Laurel's thoughts continued into the danger zone, Stella set aside her plate, settled into the bed and closed her eyes. "I'm going to take a little nap, dears. But you two stay and chatter on. You won't bother me a bit."

"Take a nap if you want to, Princess," he said in a low tone. "I'll hang around to make sure Stella's really okay." He must have seen wariness in her expression. "Don't worry, I won't jump on you while you're sleeping. That robe of yours sets me on fire, but I'll hold back.''

"Thanks for your consideration, Wade, but I don't need a nap.'' She wished he'd go. Wished even more he'd stay.

"If you're not sleepy, why don't I teach you to use chopsticks? The secret is to hold the top stick like a pencil.'' He maneuvered the wooden rod easily, picking up single grains of rice. "Give it a try.''

She grasped her chopsticks in her own awkward fashion, moved them in clumsy jabs.

"Like this, Princess.'' He took her hand, gently shook her fingers free from their cramped grip, then massaged them to ease the tension.

She drew a sharp breath at the unexpected contact of his large, warm hands as he placed her fingers on the chopstick. She wanted to pull away, but was loath to let him know how much his touch affected her. Willing her hand to remain perfectly still, she held her body stiffly.

"Relax. These little pieces of wood won't fight back, and the bottom one just rests along your thumb.'' He slipped the second stick in place. As Stella snored gently, Wade continued his instructions. With practice, Laurel's skills improved. She lifted a snow pea to her mouth, depositing only a small smear of sauce on her cheek in the process. She chewed the now cold food as though it were ambrosia, relishing her triumph.

"I think you've got it,'' he announced with the pride of a teacher whose slowest student had mastered a difficult task. He wiped the sauce from her cheek with a paper napkin, his face so near that she felt his breath ruffle the fine hair at her temple.

Disconcerted, she made a grab for a piece of chicken that promptly slithered from between the chopsticks and skittered onto the table.

"I think you've lost it," he said solemnly, humor lighting his eyes.

Laurel hated to fail at anything. "I'll show you who's lost it." Carefully repositioning her fingers, she tried to pick up another piece of chicken but ended up chasing it around the plate.

"I can't stand to watch you torment that helpless hunk of poultry." Wade lifted it with his chopsticks and raised it to her lips.

She opened her mouth slowly, reluctant to let him feed her, wary of the intimacy of that act. Yet she couldn't turn away. She accepted the food, closing her eyes to shut out the warmth in his gaze, to tamp down the tingling sensations spreading within her.

Blast him. He was as changeable as a chameleon. Sarcastic and insulting one moment, gently teasing the next. She'd make the most of this pleasant moment with him before he reverted to his Mr. Hyde persona.

She worked with the chopsticks with renewed vigor, laughing softly with him at her clumsy efforts, earning a murmur of admiration with each success. He didn't try to feed her again, a fact that should have pleased her but didn't.

When she'd cleaned her plate, he checked his watch. "I guess I'll go to my room. I need to make a phone call."

She stopped herself just before asking, "Checking with your bookie?" He'd been too kind, too caring to deserve her taunts today. Tomorrow would be another day, another opportunity to distance herself from Wade.

He stood and watched Stella for a moment, then, apparently satisfied with her condition, headed for the door. "I left a couple of sandwiches and a carton of fruit salad in the ice chest if you get hungry later. I'll see you tomorrow."

What was happening here? She and Wade had been together for an hour without exchanging insults. Not good. She needed to gird herself against his onslaught. Keep her verbal weapons sharpened and ready.

After tossing and turning for hours, Laurel gave up on sleep for the night. To keep from disturbing Stella's rest, she left the bed, opened the drapes and sat in a chair beside the fly-specked window.

The pale half moon hung in the hazy sky above the parking lot, its silvery light filtering into the room. A romantic night. A night for lovers. If one *had* a lover. Ah, well, she set that thought aside. She didn't have time for a lover, didn't want one.

That wasn't quite true. She would like to share her life with a loving man, one who'd encourage her, share his own dreams and goals with her. But she had no prospects, and she had no interest in an affair.

She wasn't a woman of the nineties, able to go from man to man without a commitment, without a regret. So she slept alone, not counting these three weeks of sharing lumpy beds with her gently snoring aunt, she thought wryly.

She'd wanted Wade since she'd first discovered desire. She would probably die wanting him, the one man who should have Wrong Choice stamped on his forehead. She had only to remember that night twelve years ago when he'd seduced her, then humiliated her.

She'd initiated that intimacy, she reluctantly admitted to herself, stirring up painful memories like one who couldn't resist worrying an achy tooth with a probing tongue. She'd looked for him until she'd found him, shirtless, working in Homer's toolshed. Barechested and sweaty, sexy and dangerous. *No good.*

She'd asked him to kiss her, but she'd wanted much more than her first major kiss. She'd wanted him to make love to her. She was tired of being the only virgin in the junior class, and what better way to solve the problem of having nothing to say when late-night discussions at her dorm turned to sexual adventures?

She'd had no concept of what she'd sought, of the depth of need she would unleash in herself with her ardent aggression.

But Wade was older, a man, not a teenager, and he'd taken advantage of her innocence. He'd kissed her obligingly, ravaging her mouth, then stroked her breasts until she was wild with need and begged him to take her.

Then, in a moment of monstrous cruelty, he'd pushed her away, told her she wasn't woman enough for him and left her alone with her tangled emotions.

All he'd taken were her dignity and her pride.

And he could do it again. But only if she let him.

She wouldn't. She couldn't face the prospect of living with fresh hurt, callously inflicted, then left to fester painfully in her heart for another twelve years.

Chapter Six

God was punishing him for something. Wade was sure of it.

He slammed down the hood of Stella's car, taking perverse pleasure in the shriek of protesting metal. He wanted to shout curses at the vast desert sky in hopes that God would get the message: he'd punished Wade Taggart enough.

"The radiator's dry, Stella," he said mildly instead. "It must have sprung a leak."

"We have plenty of ice, a dozen cans of cola and all that lovely beverage you bought, dear. Won't that take care of your little problem?"

"There's not enough liquid to be of real help, and we need it to drink." Besides, he figured the cola contained enough acid to eat through the radiator.

His "little problem" went beyond an empty radiator on a lonely New Mexico road at high noon. Thoughts of Laurel had kept him awake last night.

Every time he'd closed his eyes, he'd seen her: lovely, haughty, laughing, insulting—but never boring, even in that silly blue robe. And beneath that changeable surface, he'd sensed vulnerability, pain. He'd wanted to wrap his arms around her, pull the pins from her prim topknot and let her hair sift through his fingers. He'd wanted to kiss her again, feast on her mouth, take her to his bed and make love to every inch of her enticing body.

He was a fool to torture himself with thoughts of making love with her. He couldn't even afford to look at her. Not in what she was wearing today—a skirt so short it hid almost nothing of her long, tanned legs. Glorious, shapely legs. A metallic red blouse clung lovingly to her breasts.

He wondered why she'd decided to display herself the day after they'd spent "quality time" together, talking with each other without exchanging insults and accusations. He'd hoped that she would at least lay off the barbs for the rest of the trip.

Instead, she'd chosen to tempt him with scanty clothes. Without a word about it, she'd just strolled coolly from her room, carrying her suitcase, the envelope with her lesson plans and the urn. She'd settled herself in the seat beside him and shot him a glare that dared him to comment.

She knew what she was doing to him, he was sure of that, wearing a sexy outfit, yet acting angry with him for looking at her. He could look, but he couldn't touch. No, he couldn't even look.

He could fantasize, though.

He cast his gaze heavenward again. *Thanks a lot, God.*

He didn't have time to ponder about the princess. What Stella described as his "little problem" loomed very large. He was responsible for their safety, and here they were, stranded somewhere in Guadalupe County, New Mexico, on a little-used, two-lane road. There wasn't much he could do to protect them from the blast furnace heat and the uncertainty of rescue, but he had to try.

He considered hiking down the road in search of help, but he couldn't recall when they'd passed a house, much less a repair shop. The map revealed no hint of civilization within walking distance in the other direction. Chances were, he'd end up buzzard bait before he found help. Besides, leaving Stella and the princess alone by the roadside might put them in greater danger if they were discovered.

If no one picked them up by dark, when the temperature dropped, he'd think again about searching for help. Meanwhile, he'd do what he could. He dragged the ice chest from the back seat and set it in the narrow band of shade created by the car's shadow. He hauled his duffel bag from the trunk and laid it on the ground by the car door, forming a crude bench.

"Okay, ladies. I want you to sit here with the ice chest lid open and the fan blowing on you. That's the best I can do to keep you from frying."

Laurel plopped on her straw hat, leaving the long ties dangling, and sat on one corner of the duffel bag without a word, without meeting his eyes. Without acknowledging that she knew how enticing she looked.

Stella sat on the opposite end, opened her parasol and tugged her skirt up to her knees, revealing the bandages that reminded him of yesterday's near disaster. He *had* to take better care of her.

Stella studied him from behind her heart-shaped sunglasses, then volunteered, "Don't worry, dear. Homer and I had car trouble lots of times, and someone always found us. We'll be fine."

While he was gratified that her spunk was intact, he admitted he might strangle her if she used the words *wonderful adventure,* to describe this debacle.

She patted the space between them. "Sit here, dear, while we wait for someone to rescue us."

He eyed the narrow space. No way would he squeeze himself into that spot, rubbing his body against Laurel's nearly bare one. "I'll stand beside the car and try to flag someone down. Keep taking small sips of thirst quencher and sucking on ice chips."

Laurel eyed him critically from scalp to toes. "Who do you think would pick up someone who looks like you?"

"Serial killers, maybe?" Her eyes widened, pleasing him enormously.

When Stella deemed it lunchtime, she prepared another round of PBJ sandwiches and handed around colas. "We're dining al fresco today, my dears."

He was thirsty, thanks to the heavily salted sausage he had managed to eat for breakfast and the peanut butter that clung to the roof of his mouth, but he held back from drinking more than a few sips of the odious cola, not knowing how long they might be stuck in this godforsaken place.

He should have been better prepared for this turn of events. He'd had another mechanic work on the car in Amarillo yesterday, replacing the worn parts that still remained after the first round of repairs. Checking the radiator was the mechanic's responsibility, but Wade should have thought to check it himself. If he had, perhaps they wouldn't be stuck here.

For two hours he paced several yards from the car, his bush hat providing scant respite from the sun. The sweatband rubbed against his scar, irritating the sutures until they itched relentlessly. The wound had nearly healed so the stitches no longer served a purpose, except to drive him crazy.

And his jeans encased his legs in a sauna. Maybe he could do something about that, at least. "Do you have scissors buried in that huge purse, Stell?" Looking puzzled, she snagged a vicious looking pair from her bag and handed them over. "I'm going to convert these pants into shorts," he explained, carefully poking the pointed blade through heavy denim.

"Don't cut off anything valuable, dear," she admonished, snapping his picture as he glanced up, startled. His hand jerked, carving a four-inch scratch on his upper thigh. He bit off a curse and shot a long look at Laurel who was watching him intently, her lips slightly parted.

"I could use a little help here, Princess," he drawled lasciviously. "Care to cut my pants off?"

"If I had the scissors and the opportunity," she said too sweetly, "I'd cut off something besides your pants, Wade."

Score one for the princess. But he liked the way she looked at him, observing his every move. He might as well give her a show. She had one coming. He turned sideways, tightened his buttocks and bent down, treating her to a view of his rear end. He thought he heard a sharp intake of breath.

Sexual frustration drove men to perform amazingly stupid stunts.

The denim resisted his efforts to cut it, so he made a show of tugging at it, flexing his arm muscles in the process. After a while, he paused for a languorous stretch and glanced at Laurel. Watching his every move, she traced her lips with the tip of her tongue. Oh, yeah, he was getting to her.

Then he remembered she was dehydrated. She'd moistened her lips to soothe them from the dry heat.

"Isn't Wade handsome, dear?" Stella asked. *Bless the woman!* "He reminds me of a lot of Phil. Same build, same coloring, but your ex wasn't as sexy."

He couldn't resist. "Do you think I'm sexy, Princess?"

"*Some* women might think so," Laurel muttered.

Score two for the princess. But she'd nearly choked on the words. Something seemed to be wrong with her breathing, he thought, smirking to himself. Served her right.

"Did you know Laurel had been married?" Stella asked, jerking him out of his thoughts.

"Uh-huh," he said, barely managing a bored tone. Oh, yeah, he knew. Stella had told him. He remembered the date of the wedding. He also remembered getting stinking drunk that night to ease the ache in his chest. He'd accepted then, with finality, that he would never have Laurel Covington.

Once he'd survived his monumental hangover, he'd begun working harder than he'd ever planned to, because complicated, mind-absorbing work kept him from thinking about his loneliness, his rootlessness.

Yet, there she sat twelve years later, lost with him in the desert, driving him nuts with her skimpy clothes and sharp tongue.

No matter what his sins had been, he didn't deserve this.

"What ever happened to Phil, dear?" Stella asked.

He didn't want to hear about the object of Laurel's affection, but curiosity got the best of him. He finished cutting the legs off his jeans and gave up any pretense of not listening.

"I don't know where he is, and I really don't care," she said tonelessly. "Things just didn't work out between us. The marriage didn't last very long."

"So you packed up and went home to Daddy?" he asked.

"I packed up and went to Edgarville," she said, "and got on with my life."

"You just walked out on the poor sucker?"

She chewed on her lower lip for a moment. "You might say that."

It figured, of course. All her life she'd been given everything she wanted. She'd never had to struggle for anything. So when her marriage got in trouble, she'd walked away rather than hanging in and trying to fix it.

She would do it again, he reminded himself. Not that he needed to worry. There was zero chance she'd ever marry him—or that he'd even want to marry her, he argued, squelching the disappointment that zinged through him. The best defense being a strong offense, he decided to keep on taunting her.

"So, Princess, are you looking for a replacement?" he asked lightly. He strutted a couple of steps in her direction and gave her a mock leer. "I could add some excitement to your life."

"I don't want excitement," she said stoutly, though she averted her gaze. "I want a man I can rely on. A man I'd be comfortable with, and that type is in short supply."

"Ah, you're searching for Mr. Comfortable. Someone who's rich and steady. A merger of fortunes and boring lives."

"What I'm looking for is none of your business."

"Now, dears, don't let's fight," Stella chided. "We're supposed to be having the time of our lives, and you two are ruining it with your silly bickering."

"You're right, of course," he admitted as Laurel nodded in agreement.

Oppressed by the heat and the silence, he strolled fifty feet down the road, needing physical distance from Laurel. Squinting at the horizon where the straight, flat, two-lane road stretched toward infinity in both directions, he hoped for some sign of life.

Nothing. Three hundred and sixty degrees of nothing except sand and clumps of dry grass, ground-hugging shrubs and cactus. Paradise.

"Wade." Laurel's soft voice came from behind him. "I'm worried about Stella. How long can we last out here?"

He couldn't resist gallows humor. "Who knows, Princess? I've never been stranded on a desert island before, and basically that's where we are." He added a grim tone to his voice. "The real question is, how long will it take for someone to find our bodies? Probably long after the buzzards have picked us clean."

She sucked in a quick breath and glanced at the sky. He watched fear darken her eyes. Her mouth worked silently, and he thought for a moment she might cry.

"Some source of strength and common sense you are," she said gamely and managed a semblance of a

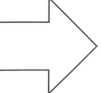

NO COST! NO OBLIGATION TO BUY! NO PURCHASE NECESSARY!

PLAY "LUCKY 7" AND GET FIVE FREE GIFTS!

HOW TO PLAY:

1. With a coin, carefully scratch off the silver box at the right. Then check the claim chart to see what we have for you—FREE BOOKS and a gift—ALL YOURS! ALL FREE!

2. Send back this card and you'll receive brand-new Silhouette Romance™ novels. These books have a cover price of $3.25 each, but they are yours to keep absolutely free.

3. There's no catch. You're under no obligation to buy anything. We charge nothing—ZERO—for your first shipment. And you don't have to make any minimum number of purchases—not even one!

4. The fact is thousands of readers enjoy receiving books by mail from the Silhouette Reader Service™ months before they're available in stores. They like the convenience of home delivery and they love our discount prices!

5. We hope that after receiving your free books you'll want to remain a subscriber. But the choice is yours—to continue or cancel, anytime at all! So why not take us up on our invitation, with no risk of any kind. You'll be glad you did!

This beautiful porcelain box is topped with a lovely bouquet of porcelain flowers, perfect for holding rings, pins or other precious trinkets — and is yours absolutely free when you accept our no risk offer!

PLAY "LUCKY 7"

**Just scratch off the silver box with a coin.
Then check below to see the gifts you get.**

YES! I have scratched off the silver box. Please send me all the gifts for which I qualify. I understand I am under no obligation to purchase any books, as explained on the back and on the opposite page.

215 CIS A3H9
(U-SIL-R-08/96)

NAME

ADDRESS   APT.

CITY   STATE   ZIP

7 7 7	**WORTH FOUR FREE BOOKS PLUS A FREE PORCELAIN TRINKET BOX**
🍒🍒🍒	**WORTH THREE FREE BOOKS**
⬤⬤⬤	**WORTH TWO FREE BOOKS**
🔔🔔🍒	**WORTH ONE FREE BOOK**

Offer limited to one per household and not valid to current Silhouette Romance™ subscribers. All orders subject to approval.

PRINTED IN U.S.A.

THE SILHOUETTE READER SERVICE™: HERE'S HOW IT WORKS

Accepting free books places you under no obligation to buy anything. You may keep the books and gift and return the shipping statement marked "cancel". If you do not cancel, about a month later we'll send you 6 additional novels, and bill you just $2.67 each plus 25¢ delivery and applicable sales tax, if any.* That's the complete price—and compared to cover prices of $3.25 each—quite a bargain! You may cancel at any time, but if you choose to continue, every month we'll send you 6 more books, which you may either purchase at the discount price…or return to us and cancel your subscription.

*Terms and prices subject to change without notice. Sales tax applicable in N.Y.

smile. "Isn't that the only reason Aunt Stella invited you?"

"That and my incredible hitchhiking skills."

"So dazzle me. Conjure up a stretch limo, air-conditioned, of course, with gallons of ice water, a swimming pool, chilled champagne, Dennis Quaid behind the wheel . . ."

He squinted against the sun, blinked and squinted again, hope rising in his heart.

"Your wish is my command, Princess. Methinks a chariot doth approach."

Shielding her eyes, she stared down the road. "Something's moving, but don't get your hopes up, it might only be a dust devil."

He trotted to the center of the road, waving both arms like semaphore flags, feeling a little foolish since the vehicle was still a speck in the distance.

Minutes later an ancient green pickup, its bed burdened with towering wooden crates of chickens, rattled toward them. The elderly driver slowed, looked them over, ground to a halt and consulted with his female passenger in a swift flurry of Spanish.

"My chariot, I presume?" Laurel looked more worried than pleased. Perhaps this lowly means of transportation wasn't good enough for her.

"Oh, my." Stella joined them beside the road, camera at the ready, smiling broadly. "Saved by a truckload of chickens. Isn't this a wonderful adventure?"

The driver rolled down his window. *"¿A donde van, señor?"*

If only he could communicate with the man. He'd learned rudimentary French and German as business necessities, but his Spanish was limited to long-ago high school courses. He approached the driver, concentrating on appearing nonthreatening. "Uh, *señor, por favor, me amigos...*" Now what? He waved toward Stella's car, then the horizon, wishing he'd stayed awake in Spanish class.

Hesitantly Laurel crept closer to the truck and flashed her million-dollar smile at the man and woman. *"Buenos dias, señor y señora."* Speaking rapidly and without hesitation, she described their predicament. At least he thought so, judging by her gestures.

The man and woman smiled in unison, black eyes sparkling, and the driver spoke. *"De seguro, señora."*

"They'll give us a ride to a garage up the road," she said, then introduced Santos and Gloria Hernandez. Stella smiled and began speaking cheerfully in English. Gloria responded in Spanish. Neither seemed aware of any language barrier.

"Bring me the ashes, dear," Stella said to him. "They'll be safer with me."

He brought her the urn, then pulled the thirst quencher and colas from the ice chest, stowed it and his duffel bag in the car and locked it. All the while he mused at this new aspect of Laurel as she chatted comfortably with two poor, Spanish-speaking chicken ranchers. Hardly her usual milieu. Then he remembered that she taught school in Edgarville, where many people spoke no English, and most Anglos never learned Spanish.

But Laurel had. He *hated* discovering that she had so many admirable qualities.

As he helped Stella into the cab of the pickup and placed the drinks on the floor, the Hernandezes laughed. The princess must have told a joke at his expense, for the couple eyed him, grinning merrily.

"¿No es su esposa?" Gloria asked.

Not your husband, Wade translated, proud of his near bilingualism.

"Ay! No!" Laurel pointed to her temple, as though the mere thought was unthinkable. *"Es loco, señora."*

Crazy. Well, yes, and Laurel Covington had made him that way. He'd been a perfectly content businessman when he'd started this trip four long days ago.

"Muy loco. Es la señorita," he said, stretching the limits of his Spanish.

Gloria dramatically clutched her hands to her heart. "Ahh, *enamorado,"* she sighed.

Laurel shook her head vigorously and strode to the truck's bed, her smile fading. She stepped on the running board and swung one leg then the other over the side, exposing every inch of her damnably sexy legs for a brief moment. Standing up in the truck bed, she glanced down at her microskirt, then shot an angry look at him as though she'd read his mind.

He shrugged elaborately. "Don't blame me, Princess. I didn't force you to wear that outfit." When she huffed, he leered and added, "But I'm glad you did."

"Get in the truck and shut up, Wade."

He mock complained. "But, Princess, the chickens aren't even potty trained." Climbing aboard, he spread the newspapers Santos had provided and knelt in the small vacant space among the crates of raucous, smelly chickens.

"Sit down, Princess, if you can in that skirt."

"Aunt Stella bought these clothes for me, so I have to wear them whether I want to or not," she snapped. With another dark glare, she angled her legs awkwardly and sank onto the newspapers, her nose within a foot of his, her bare, satiny thigh pressed against his hair-roughened leg.

Lord, she was too sexy for his own good.

She gasped, turned her head and sneezed—a mighty, honking blast that stunned the chickens into momentary silence, followed by agitated clucking.

"I'm alerdic to fedders," she explained through blocked sinuses while snagging a bottle of allergy pills from her purse.

"Why didn't you say something?"

"Ad make At Stella squat back here with you? Or wait for better tradsportation? I bay be a pridcess, but I'b dot stupid," she groused in her new dialect. She opened a cola can and slugged down two pills.

"It's all right," she continued, "Whed we get booving, the fresh air will help."

The truck lurched forward, then jounced along the road at the same pace as Stella's car. The breeze snatched Laurel's hat, whirled it out of the truck and sent it tumbling end-over-end across the desert.

"Oh, dabit!"

Laurel looked so cute and harmless with her red nose, watery eyes, impaired speech and skimpy clothes, that he confided in her without thinking.

"I hate that car of Stell's, worrying all the time about safety. I'd like to buy her a decent car, but traveling on the brink of disaster in that old wreck is so important to her. I'm afraid I'd hurt her feelings, her pride, if I forced a better car on her."

"You'd probably have to steal wud. You look like a plastic bodel is all you could afford."

Forget *cute and harmless*. Allergies made her meaner than ever. He'd had it with her assumptions about him.

"For your information, Princess," he said, his tone deliberately harsh, "I haven't stolen anything since I was thirteen and liberated a ten-speed bicycle. When

Homer found out, he told me he'd take a strip off my hide if I ever pulled such a stupid stunt again." His voice gentled at the memory of Homer. "He scared me straight, because I worshipped that old man and would rather have died than lose his respect."

He glanced tenderly at Stella through the rear window and continued, wondering how the princess would react to this baring of his soul. "Stell went with me when I returned the bike and stumbled through an apology. She kept her hand on my shoulder, silently supporting and encouraging me to do the right thing. Lord, I worship that woman. She and Homer were the only people who ever really loved me."

"Why did you steal the bike?" she asked matter-of-factly, then blew her nose. She looked curious, rather than condemning, an encouraging sign.

"The easy answer is that I wanted a bike as good as the other kids had."

"That's not a reason—"

"Of course not. It took me years to understand the real reason. I'd run away, and my father was too drunk to try to stop me. I hitchhiked for three days to get to Stell's, the only place I knew I'd be accepted. She fed me, hugged me, gave me a safe place to sleep and didn't ask many questions, bless her heart. But she also enrolled me in summer school, and I was frustrated with having to play catch-up with my education. I was the new kid again, the one who was way behind in math. The dumb one. The one who got into fights, won most of them and was condemned for it by parents and teachers. So I stole a bike to get even with the world."

There. He'd exposed his hurt, his vulnerability to Laurel Covington, whose biggest childhood problem was deciding which dress to wear to the prom. Who'd probably never even considered stealing so much as a piece of gum. He straightened his spine, ready for her sarcasm, a lecture on morality, or worse, her pity.

"That was the summer when you were thirteen and I was ten?"

He nodded, wondering where she was heading, and pleased that her allergy medicine seemed to be working.

"A couple of weeks later you disrupted my birthday party and smeared ice cream all over me."

Trust her to focus on herself. "Sorry, Princess, but you were a rich, spoiled kid—part of the world I wanted to get even with. I was jealous of you."

"I had wealthy parents who gave me every material thing I wanted. I had no idea what the rest of the world was like. At the time, I knew you were, according to my father, a young hoodlum who stole bicycles and ruined birthday parties."

"Only on my best days, Princess." Grateful that he'd escaped unscathed from the discussion thus far, he changed the subject. "You're getting sunburned." She fished around in her purse and pulled out a tube of sun block.

"That will help, but you need to get out of the sun."

She looked around the truck bed and raised a questioning eyebrow.

"Here." He peeled off his T-shirt and draped it over her head and shoulders. "Not as good as a beach umbrella, but better than a chicken crate."

He took the sun block from her and squeezed lotion on his fingertips. Holding his breath, wondering if she'd accept his touch, he spread warm, creamy lotion on her arms and shoulders, never taking his eyes from hers. She watched him watch her. Even her sunglasses couldn't hide her wide eyes—uncertain, wary, but unresisting.

He replenished the lotion and brushed it over the warm, soft skin of her face. The pulse at the base of her throat jumped, its pace accelerating. He drew back, absently rubbing his hands over his chest to wipe off the remaining sun block. Slowly raising his hands, he lifted her sunglasses away so he could see into the depths of her blue eyes, his fingertips brushing the fine, golden hair at her temples.

She closed her eyes against the sudden glare, her full lips softly drawn into an *O*. Then, blinking slowly, her long, dark lashes fanning her cheeks, she removed his sunglasses and looked deep into his eyes. Into his soul.

He was going to kiss her. He knew it—knew he couldn't resist the urgency that hardened his body and ruled his mind.

This was the ideal place to kiss Laurel Covington, he thought wryly. He couldn't lose control, couldn't give in fully to his desires. Surrounded by crates of raucous, malodorous chickens, in full view of his beloved aunt, he could safely kiss red-nosed, sniffling Laurel. He couldn't touch her, would only allow himself a small taste of her lips to assuage the need that had been building in him since he'd driven into Stella's driveway. This kiss would be sweet and simple. He was sure of it.

He was wrong.

Wade was going to kiss her. Laurel knew it—knew she should resist—but need tugged deep inside her. Eyes dark as midnight held hers in thrall...black, windblown hair...compellingly handsome, masculine face. He was the sexiest man alive.

She wanted his kiss, despite the risk of carelessly inflicted pain. He'd used his shirt to shelter her, baring his broad, tanned chest with its sculpted muscles for her leisurely, close-up inspection. He'd aroused her by simply spreading lotion on her arms and face, touching her hair, removing her sunglasses, leaving her vulnerable. She wondered what this kiss would be like, as he bent toward her.

He brushed his lips against hers, creating a sweet, warm friction, then traced her lips with the tip of his tongue, soothing away the heat. He kissed and soothed, again and again. She wanted to slide her arms around his neck and pull him closer but feared letting him know how much she wanted this intimacy.

Feared letting herself know.

The tip of his tongue dipped between her lips, seeking entrance that she had no thought of refusing. He explored her mouth, his tongue darting, probing. Savoring the taste of him, the heady scent of him, she responded with explorations of her own, loving the soft warmth of his mouth, the delicate tingles drifting through her breasts, swirling through her veins.

She couldn't remember a kiss like this, one that made her feel cherished. She wanted to prolong it, to revel in it. This was how he should have kissed her twelve years ago, she thought dimly, as she gave herself up to the pleasures of kissing Wade Taggart.

Finally Wade put his hands on her shoulders and slowly lifted his head, breaking the sensual tension mounting between them. He sat back on his heels, averting his gaze.

"That was a mistake. Sorry, Princess," he said diffidently, as if nothing had happened. Nothing that mattered.

Blast! "We seem to make the same mistake every twelve years," she said, hoping he wouldn't hear the tiny quaver in her voice that bespoke this new humiliation. Blast him for kissing her so tenderly, seeking nothing but pleasure, demanding nothing but that she share it, then shrugging it off as a mistake. He was *sorry* he'd kissed her!

She should be sorry, too. She had no business kissing him. Blowing her nose, more to have something to do than from real need, she forced herself to prepare lesson plans in her mind so she could avoid looking at him, noticing how close their bodies were and that apparently he had nothing more to say to her. But making a list of words that start with the *B* sound, a supremely boring activity, didn't help at all.

She needed desperately to be out of sight, and sound, and scent, of Wade Taggart. Avoiding his gaze was no problem because he was studying a crate of chickens as though he'd had a lifelong interest in poultry transportation.

She squirmed backward, hoping to increase the distance between them, but succeeded only in generating a wave of heat when her thigh slid along his. Stella chose that moment to take a picture through the rear window. Terrific.

In a half hour the pickup ground to a halt beside an ancient gas pump. With a sigh of relief that she echoed, Wade leapt from the truck. He introduced himself to Joe Nieto, who identified himself as the owner of the establishment, then described their problem.

Laurel straightened her cramped legs, sneezed and stood up unsteadily in the truck bed for a minute until she regained strength in her numb limbs. She surveyed the small town that consisted of a few weatherbeaten frame houses with most of their paint peeled off by the merciless heat; a dilapidated, six-room motel that only Stella could love; and a Mexican food café that most certainly served the haute cuisine of the trip—fat, cholesterol and salt.

"Sure, I can tow your car in, and I'm a pretty fair mechanic," Joe assured them, "except for those high tech computers they put on fancy cars these days."

"This car may predate computers," Wade said, handing him the keys to Stella's car. "You'll recognize it. It's lemon yellow."

Laurel climbed from the truck as decorously as her skirt would permit, immensely grateful that the next step in their rescue seemed assured.

Wade paid Joe for the gas Santos pumped into his pickup, a nice gesture, Laurel thought. As they thanked the Hernandezes, the couple dutifully posed for Stella's camera, then drove away.

With nothing to do but wait for Joe to return, the three of them settled inside the station. Laurel and Stella shared a hard wooden bench directly across from the ancient, wheezing evaporative cooler that blew blessedly chilly, damp wind over them, bringing heavenly relief from the baking heat.

Stella pulled a cigarette from her bag and tried valiantly to light it. The fast-moving air current defeated each effort until she sighed and gave up.

Three feet away Wade perched his hip on the battered desk and studied the array of auto parts hanging from wall pegs. He caught Laurel glancing at him, their gazes locking for an electrifying second before she looked away, feeling as though she'd given up on a personal contest with him.

He was sorry he'd kissed her.

She was, too, but for different reasons.

"Laurel, why don't you tell Wade about your exciting project?" Stella said, breaking the tense silence.

Oh, right. Wade was the last person she wanted to confide in, especially after he'd leapt to the wrong conclusions about the failure of her marriage. Conclusions she'd not challenged because the truth was too humiliating.

Her plans were so dear to her heart, too, a goal she spent most of her free time on. She hated to expose her dreams to his sarcasm.

"I don't think he'd be interested," she said, ignoring the fact that he was in the room and capable of speaking for himself.

"Of course he would, dear. And he could help you with it, couldn't you, Wade?"

"Sure, Stell, I can fix anything," he said. His self-deprecating half grin lacked real humor. "So, what are you up to, Princess? It's not this Antibes thing again, is it? I've already heard about the trip with the fabulous Lubster."

What in the world...? Oh, yes, her fictitious boyfriend. "What about him? And his name is Lud," she corrected, delighted to pluck the word from her memory.

"Are we going to hear more about him?" he asked sourly, eyes glinting.

For an instant she thought he was jealous. Ridiculous, she chided herself. Wade was sorry he'd kissed her. Why would he care if she had a boyfriend? Anxious to change the subject, she drew a breath and plunged into her story.

"I want to start an adult literacy center in Edgarville. It's badly needed. Some people can read Spanish but not English. Others are so illiterate that they can't fill out job applications or read even the simplest printed instructions.

"Parents can't help their kids with their homework, so the kids get behind, and too many of them drop out before they learn to read adequately. It's a cycle of lost opportunities, and I want to help break it."

Oh, Lordy, she sounded sanctimonious. She couldn't help it. She wanted so much for the poor people in her adopted hometown. And for many of them, reading was the key to a better job, a more secure future.

Stella smiled at her proudly, then turned to Wade. "Isn't Laurel wonderful, dear?" she asked sweetly. "She does so much for her students, and now she's going to help their parents, too."

"She's a swell example for all mankind," he assured her, his sarcasm sailing over Stella's head and slamming like a fist into Laurel's heart. His mocking gaze fixed on her, he added, "So, Princess, what are you waiting for?"

She was waiting for money. Money for rent, money for furniture, money for computers, money for supplies, insurance, advertising, and on and on. Lots of money.

"I've applied for several grants, and I'm waiting to hear. But I'll also need sponsors who'll agree to make regular contributions and who aren't interested in turning a profit—at least not in the form of cash. I'm working on that, contacting people I used—people I know."

"You aren't using your own money, Princess? Seems like you could build and equip your own place."

"Are you kid—!" She stopped just short of shouting, "I have no money, you idiot!" He thought she was still rich; he was *supposed* to think so.

"I'm setting aside some money," she said lamely. Every bit she could save from her small salary, but that would never be enough. "I'm working with a few new readers at my apartment and designing curriculum in my spare time." Darn it, she sounded apologetic about her efforts.

He persisted. "You could endow the center yourself and call it The Laurel Covington Center for Misguided Do-Gooders."

"Misguided? Do-gooders?" she shouted, jumping to her feet. "Who the hell are *you* to criticize me, to mock me for helping people? What have you ever done for anyone?"

For an instant she considered strangling him with one of the radiator belts hanging from the wall. His worthless life was spared by the reappearance of Joe's truck, with Stella's heap rattling along in tow.

Laurel sat down next to her aunt, drawing deep breaths to calm herself. "I'm sorry for my bad language, Aunt Stella, but he made me so mad."

"It's all right, dear." Stella patted her hand sympathetically. "I thought you had a damn good point." Ignoring Laurel's gasp and smothered giggle, she turned to Wade and said earnestly, "You could help her with the business stuff, couldn't you, dear?"

"I don't think she'd want my input," he said, never so much as flicking a glance at Laurel. "Besides, why would I want to get involved with the princess on any level?"

Without waiting for the derisive snort she was preparing, he stalked outside and spoke with Joe.

"Wade really likes you," Stella announced as the door closed. "I think your new clothes are paying off." She gave Laurel a knowing wink.

"Aunt Stella, he doesn't like me. In fact, he can't stand me, and it's getting worse, not better." *He's sorry he kissed me.* "Besides, I don't like him. You heard how he mocked me and my plans. Why would I want another man like that? Phil was more than enough."

Stella fished around in her bag and pulled out the day's photographic efforts. "Here. Look at this one. Isn't it sweet?"

Laurel saw herself with Wade's shirt draped over her head and shoulders, sunglasses in her hand, her head turned away from him. He stared blankly past the camera as though unaware of it, his face bleak.

"Think again about the picture, Aunt Stella. We can't even stand to look at each other."

Stella beamed. "Exactly. You can tell people are in love by the way they look at each other, of course. But you can *really* tell it when two people are carefully *not* looking at each other. You and Wade are definitely not looking at each other."

"Wade was just plain bored. In my case, you're seeing the effects of allergies."

With a "harrumph" of displeasure, her aunt flourished another picture. "There, that proves it. Look at the way you two are kissing."

Oh, yeah, just look. They seemed so caught up in each other, oblivious to their ridiculous surroundings. But she was the only one whose emotions were tangled by the kiss—and the kiss off.

"It's a kiss, all right. But he apologized for it."

"Apologized? The young fool." She shoved the pictures into her purse and drew out a cigarette and lighter. Ducking into a corner of the room, her back to the fan, she managed to light the cigarette. She returned to her seat and blew a cloud of smoke in Laurel's direction.

"Stubborn, stubborn, stubborn," she muttered between puffs, her voice barely audible above the whooshing roar of the evaporative cooler.

While Laurel pondered whether to respond to Stella's comment, Joe and Wade walked into the office.

"I can definitely fix the radiator leak, ladies, no problem." Laurel went weak with relief. The sooner they could move on, the quicker Stella's mission would be completed, leaving Laurel to return to her normal life.

Joe checked the wall clock and continued, "I'll do it tomorrow. My quittin' time is five, and it's ten after."

"Couldn't you work overtime this once?" Laurel pleaded.

"No, ma'am. I bought this place to get away from the stresses of city life after I had my bypass. Working after five stresses me."

Being stuck in this one-stop-sign town stressed Laurel. But the man's jutted chin signaled his determination to stick with his rules.

"You wouldn't happen to know about vacancies at the motel, would you?" she asked

"Of course I would. I own it. And there's two empty rooms, this being the middle of the week."

"When there are fewer tourists?" she asked in a falsely kind tone, knowing they were at the mercy of Joe Nieto, the only mechanic and hotelier within walking distance.

"How lovely to have found this place, Mr. Nieto," Stella chimed, tucking the urn into one arm and offering the other to Joe. "Perhaps you'd be so kind as to accompany us to the registration desk."

Bowing slightly, he cupped her elbow and escorted her to the motel, leaving Laurel and Wade to haul their luggage over the makeshift trail to the motel.

Tomorrow had to be better, Laurel told herself. What could be worse than this one?

Chapter Seven

"Why aren't you married, Wade, dear?" Stella asked the next morning over their breakfasts of eggs and salsa, refried beans, tortillas and bitter coffee.

"Huh?" His aunt's question interrupted his circuitous thoughts of Laurel—kissing her, caring for her, yet having nothing to offer her. Nothing she'd want, at any rate.

"It's a simple enough question, dear," Stella said patiently. "Why aren't you married?"

A man ought to be able to finish his breakfast and his morning's pointless ruminations about the woman who was driving him nuts, before being asked such a question.

"I guess it's because I never found a woman like you, Stell," he said, hoping to disarm her.

Her cheeks pinkened charmingly. "Just what is it about me that you want in a wife?"

He intended to brush off the question with a non-answer. "You're loyal, loving, determined, dependable," he said lightly.

"So is a German shepherd, dear." She lit a cigarette, sending a stream of smoke past his face, before the ceiling fan caught and disbursed the noxious fumes.

This café wasn't the place he'd have chosen to tell Stella what he loved about her, but she wanted to know, and she deserved the truth.

"You stuck with Homer through some bad times. I remember when I was eight or nine, and he lost his job." He paused to suppress the unexpected emotion that roughened his voice as he recalled the couple's quiet struggle to pay bills. "You took in a boarder, ironed clothes for the neighbors and saw me through another rough summer, all without complaining—or blaming Homer. Lots of women won't make sacrifices like that. It's easier for them to move on."

"Like your mamma did?" Stella asked softly, placing her palm over his fisted hands.

He didn't want to resurrect his past. His words had been aimed at Laurel, to needle her for walking away from her foundering marriage, abandoning her husband, without a sign of regret.

But his aunt had called to mind one of the most painful periods in his life. And she'd done so in front of the princess, the last person he wanted to know more about his emotional frailties. Yesterday's unguarded revelations had been more than enough.

He shot a glance at Laurel, curious about her reaction to another "pitiful little Wade" story. Her blue eyes were warm but not with pity. Not yet.

"How old were you?" she asked.

"Four."

"Four?" Her eyebrows drew together. "That's a hard age to lose someone you love."

He'd been four and frightened by the condemning words of his father. "It's all your fault, kid. If you'd been good, she'd have stuck around." The only good that came from his mother's desertion was that his father soon married Homer's niece and brought Stella and Homer into his life. When his stepmother died three years later, his stepgreat-aunt and -uncle remained part of his life, his only source of love, support and encouragement.

Laurel put her hand on his forearm and squeezed gently, her slim, pale fingers a stark contrast to the rougher texture of his tanned skin sprinkled with coarse, black hair.

He drew a slow breath to ease the tensions within himself. Here he sat in a public café, baring his soul to the one woman who would always love him—and to one who never would.

Maudlin, he thought, disgusted with himself. Like the tragic ending of an old B movie. He withdrew his forearms from the table, ending their public intimacy. Immediately he felt bereft of the warmth their hands had given him. Leaning against the back of his chair, arms crossed over his chest, he hoped to project a change of mood.

"To answer your question, Stell, I'm not married because I'm not good husband material," he said in a tone more lighthearted than he felt. "A wife doesn't fit into my life-style. You know I'm on the road most of the time, and I don't want to give up that freedom."

Freedom? What freedom? Freedom to travel the globe, moving from one conference room to another, always on a fast-paced schedule, always chasing a deal. Always alone. Rarely pausing to enjoy himself.

In truth, he was tired of constant travel. Of owning a condo he visited so rarely that it seemed more like a hotel than a home. But he didn't really know what his home should be like, except from Stella and Homer's example. He'd never had a home of his own where he'd felt welcomed, comfortable and comforted—the way he'd felt at visits to their home for all those years.

Sometimes he let himself think about changing his life. He pictured a loving wife who was always there for him, someone to care for, to share his life with. Someone who'd stand by him if times got tough. A fantasy life, he acknowledged, and unlikely to come true.

Setting down her coffee mug, Stella chided gently, "You'd make a wonderful husband and father, dear."

"At least as good as my old man," he said grimly, absently folding and refolding his paper napkin as he considered the crux of his fears. His father had finally run off Wade's mother by constantly blaming her for his own failures. He'd grown up bouncing from pillar to post with his old man, treated as no more than an inconvenient burden his father had resented until the day he died.

"In spite of your father," Stella maintained.

"I don't think so, Stell."

He needed to get away from Stella and Laurel, needed time to himself to think with his mind rather than his emotions. "You ladies have another cup of coffee, and I'll check on the car."

He strode rapidly toward Joe Nieto's gas station and called his office from the pay phone. He gave Marla his comments on the papers she'd faxed to him in Amarillo and told her to relay them to his client, checked up on other developments and ended the call, all without engaging his mind.

Blast Laurel Covington for distracting him. No woman had ever so attracted and annoyed him. His sweet and simple kiss had turned into something he'd rarely experienced, if at all.

Years ago her adolescent kiss had inflamed him, engulfed him with its innocent heat, a wanting to possess. Her woman's kiss had warmed him slowly, expertly, sending sweet heat drifting through his body. A longing to share his pleasure, giving and taking in equal measure, a longing so intense he'd forced himself to break away before it became a forever kiss.

Memories of that first, wild kiss had haunted him.

Yesterday's kiss scared the hell out of him, for it made him want things he could never have—not with Laurel. Permanence. Caring. Trust.

Love.

He wasn't in love with Princess Laurel. Never had been, really.

Certainly never would be.

After another bad dinner in another café that was indistinguishable from its predecessors, Wade muttered close to Laurel's ear, "We need to talk—alone."

"No, we don't." What did he want to do to her now? Reject her? Twice was enough, thank you. Mock her goals? Been there, done that. Leer at her clothes? He'd had two days' free rein with his sexy, roving eyes.

"It's nothing personal, but we've got to talk about Stella. I'll treat you to a real meal with fresh vegetables and fruit, low salt, low fat...."

"You know how to lead me down the primrose path, you silver-tongued devil," she said, pleased at her sarcastic tone.

What did he want?

"This has been a long day, what with waiting for Mr. Nieto to repair the car and then driving all this way," Stella announced. "I need my beauty sleep. You youngsters have fun tonight." She fished her room key from her purse and waved at them before entering.

"Think she overheard us?" Wade asked.

"Or read your mind, who knows?"

Wade drove to a produce stand and insisted on making the selections himself. Returning with several paper bags, he nodded his head toward a sandy, shaded area with three sagging picnic tables. Since the evening temperature had dropped to a balmy ninety degrees, she didn't argue. At least they wouldn't have to eat another meal in the car.

They sat at a table facing each other across its rough, narrow surface. With his pocket knife, he cut firm, red tomatoes into wedges and placed them on a paper plate, followed by flowerettes trimmed from a head of broccoli and bite-size chunks of zucchini and cucumbers.

"Your entrée, madame." He pushed the plate to the center of the table and picked up a piece of cucumber, munching it slowly. The twilight sky turned the clouds pink and gold at the horizon, casting his face in soft light that eased the tense lines around his eyes and mouth. He looked relaxed for the first time in days. And too appealing.

Laurel picked up a tomato wedge and savored its salty-sweet flavor. "I've gone to dietary heaven," she sighed.

His smile was warmly intimate when their fingers brushed over the plate. They ate slowly, enjoying the quiet evening breeze that rustled through the trees. When they'd finished the vegetables, he filled another plate with plump, green grapes and purple plums.

"Dessert, madame?"

"How can I refuse these tempting morsels?" She selected a plum and bit into it. The skin resisted briefly, then gave way suddenly, sending a rivulet of juice sliding from between her lips.

Before she could reach for a napkin, Wade ran his fingertip slowly from the corner of her mouth to her chin. He raised his finger to his mouth and slowly licked the drops of juice, holding her gaze with his heated one.

He was too much sensual male, staring at her with hot eyes, sucking the fingertip that had left a heated trail where he'd touched her sensitized skin.

She had to end this intimate moment. It meant nothing to Wade—and too much to her.

"What..." she croaked, then cleared her throat and continued. "What did you want to talk about? About Aunt Stella? You said..." she blabbered, trying to think about something besides the playful grin quirking up the corners of his full lips.

His face sobered. "I'm worried about her, Princess. She's always been eccentric. That's one of the things I love about her. She's always marched to her own drummer, so this mission of hers is in character. But sometimes her thinking isn't too clear."

"Like buying that awful car?" She scowled in the direction of the object of her contempt. "And smoking cigarettes again after fifty years of abstinence."

"I know she loved Uncle Homer totally, so I understand that she wants to recreate the essence of their honeymoon, even the unpleasant parts, but she's spreading his ashes in some weird places—by a particular tree or in a dank passageway. Compared to those stops, Cadillac Ranch seemed normal," Wade said. "I wonder if she's gotten confused over the years, if her memory has slipped."

She ought to mention the other possibility, even though his reply might embarrass her. "I worry about her, too, but I wonder if some of her forgetfulness is concocted. I think she's...um...matchmaking."

"Oh, yeah?"

"I'm wearing this stuff because she claims to have dropped my other outfits in the laundry chute at the Dallas motel and forgotten them. She insisted on buying this wardrobe for me."

"I never thanked her for that," Wade said, running an appreciative glance over the tiny, purple blouse that clung to her breasts.

Forcing her thoughts back to Stella's behavior, she decided to tell him about her aunt's comments, despite the reaction she expected from Wade.

"She said I needed to wear clothes like this if I wanted to..." Her voice faltered, reflecting her fear that he would humiliate her with one of his patented crude remarks. "To, um, attract a man."

His dark eyebrows arched. "Any man in particular?" he asked, his tone indicating that he knew the answer.

"You," she said, making herself look him straight in the eye.

"Why me?"

"Fishing for compliments, Wade? Even from a seventy-five-year-old woman?"

"I'll take what I can get, Princess, regardless of the source."

"She thinks you're some kind of action hero. Everything you do is perfect."

He crossed his arms over his chest. "She's right, of course," he said sardonically. "She also thinks you're Saint Laurel, the source of all that's good in the universe."

"She refuses to recognize that we don't even like each other, much less—" Her throat closed against the last words. Why was it so hard to say them, even in a negative way? Why was he watching her mouth so intently as she struggled to form the words?

"Love each other," she finally managed in a soft whisper.

"And her comments about *marriage*. I suppose she wants us to be as happy as she and Homer were," he said, not quite meeting her gaze. "But she's wasting her time trying to make us a couple, Princess. We have nothing in common."

"No kidding," she managed to say, her beliefs confirmed.

He said no more, the silence between them stretching awkwardly, while she tried to think of a different subject.

"This is hard for me to deal with," she admitted reluctantly. "I hate the thought that old age may be catching up with her. She seems to be healthy enough, but we can't be sure. Maybe there's a physical cause for her confusion. When we get home, we need to arrange for a medical evaluation so we'll know for sure."

He took her hand between both of his, offering comfort, reassurance. "I've been worried about her health, as well. If she has any serious problems, we'll help her deal with them. Even if she's all right, I need to spend more time with her, keeping up with repairs on her house. Mostly, though, I think she's lonely. She needs company." He gathered up the remains of their picnic into a paper bag and pitched it into a trash can.

"I haven't come to visit her as much as I'd have liked, either," she admitted, feeling guilty that she'd let her own interests intrude on her obligations to Stella. "In the meantime, though, we need to make sure she has a wonderful time completing her mission. It means so much to her."

"We can put up with the inconveniences, the forced togetherness, the bad food. We both love Stell enough to pretend to be having a good time for her sake." Wade stood, waiting until she joined him, then walked to the car, his hand resting on her waist, guiding her over the uneven ground in the gathering dark. "Maybe pretending won't be so hard," he added softly.

"Maybe not," she agreed with a hopeful smile. She felt safe with him, she realized. And inordinately pleased that they'd entered into an alliance, uneasy though it was, to protect Stella.

She'd lied, she admitted to herself. She *did* like some things about him. A man who cared so much about the well-being of his stepgreat-aunt must have an inner core of sensitivity and generosity, despite his efforts to hide it. He had a strong instinct to protect people he was responsible for. And a sense of humor that appealed to her, even though she was frequently the target of his jokes.

She reined in her thoughts. Liking Wade too much could only lead her into trouble—again.

Too late for warnings, she realized. For better or worse she liked Wade Taggart.

"What's new, Marla?" Wade asked distractedly, his thoughts on the evening he'd spent with Laurel. Despite all his efforts, he was falling *in like* with her. He even respected some of the things she did. Sometimes he could actually envision their becoming friends. Dangerous illusions, he knew.

He was going through a phase; he'd outgrow it.

Sure.

"...wants to talk with you about restructuring his business."

"What?" His heart skipped a beat. "I missed that."

"So how's the princess?" Marla asked instead, her tone smug and knowing.

"She's still around. Now *who* wants to talk to me?"

"Stavros—"

"I've been coaxing him for a year to restructure his shipping business. I'd nearly given up on doing a deal with him."

"Looks like you'll have to go to Athens. Boss, here's your escape hatch. Kiss your auntie goodbye, kiss off the princess and head for the nearest airport."

He'd have to leave Laurel—and Stella, too, he added as an afterthought. He could put them on a plane for Austin and be on his merry way with a promise to resume the mission in the fall when the weather would be cooler. When Laurel was busy teaching.

He'd gotten his wish, but now he wasn't so sure he wanted it. Though Laurel had confirmed that she had no romantic interest in him, as he'd always known, there'd been an unexpected sweetness about her that drew him to her. He wanted to get to know that facet of her.

"I can't abandon them," he said, quelling a resigned sigh. Not yet, at least. "I'll call Stavros and see if we can handle the preliminaries by phone and fax."

"Falling for the snotty princess, are we?" Marla cooed.

"No way. And, Marla, mind your own business."

"When have I ever done that?"

"Start now," he said, unreasonably irritated with his secretary. She was too near the mark, he realized, and he didn't want to think about it.

"Right," she said saucily. She gave him Stavros's number, reminded him of the time difference and hung up.

A couple of hours later he had a new client, and they had talked through the structure of an agreement with Stavros's attorneys and set up a schedule for telephone conferences. He should be excited about the transaction because it was complex and challenging. He ought to be completely wrapped up in the details, but they occupied only the periphery of his mind.

What would he—could he—do about Laurel?

Damned if he knew.

Heading north the next morning, Wade hoped Stella wanted to go to Santa Fe. He and Laurel could have a great time in the quaint old city, sharing a gourmet meal, wandering through art galleries and shops. Perhaps he would buy her a gift, a silver and turquoise bracelet or a piece of handmade Indian pottery.

Whoa! One semipleasant evening with the princess and he wanted to put his arm around her, take her on a romantic stroll and shower her with gifts. He'd probably even kiss her again.

Fool, he thought, hoping now that they'd bypass Santa Fe and all its seductive charms.

"Where are we heading, Stell?"

"Chaco Canyon, dear," she said between puffs of her cigarette. She consulted the map, perching her sunglasses on the top of her head and squinting. We'll turn right on Highway 44, toward Bloomfield."

"The Anasazi Indian ruins?" Laurel asked.

"Yes, dear. We'll have a wonderful adventure there."

He glanced at Laurel. She seemed more relaxed today, almost serene, as she sat with the urn clamped between her feet and watched the desert pass by her window. Today's outfit, a hot pink number that made her skin glow, was as brief and enticing as the others.

He had to admit feeling a little sympathy for her because she'd practically been forced to wear clothes that made her feel uncomfortable. He'd credit her with being a good sport and for going to great lengths to humor Stella.

She'd been quiet this morning. Perhaps she was still digesting the fact that they'd actually agreed to work together—in harmony—instead of bickering, for their aunt's sake. Laurel hadn't even balked at the prospect of cooperating with him. Or of the matchmaking. He'd have expected her to be revolted at the thought of being linked to him. But she seemed more dismayed than disgusted, which mirrored his own reaction. They were an unlikely pair, to say the least. Still . . .

Not that he'd get his hopes up. But the prospect of being on better terms with Laurel pleased him, left him anticipating a relationship based on respect and a genuine liking of each other.

Once they were on the right road, Stella announced that she would take a nap until they arrived. She settled herself so the little fan blew air across the open ice chest and toward her face, and in a few minutes she was snoring gently.

Stella took a lot of naps for a woman who claimed this trip was for her to recall the adventures of her travels with Homer, he thought. And they always seemed to coincide rather neatly with times when he and Laurel were trapped together with nothing else to do but talk.

"Oh, good heavens!" Laurel said in a harsh whisper. She turned in her seat and yanked the burning cigarette from between Stella's fingers, stubbing it out in the ashtray. "We really do need to watch her, Wade. She could have burned herself."

"Nice save, Princess." He decided to build on last night's friendly mood. "Anyone would love Stell," he began, "but why you in particular? You had parents, other close relatives and lots of friends. Why is Stell so important to you?"

She didn't answer for a moment, seeming to consider her words, then spoke hesitantly. "I spent more time with her and Homer than with my parents. Part of every summer and most holidays. Those times between boarding school and summer camp when my parents were too busy to want me around."

"You never saw your folks?"

"They'd bring me home for a few days whenever they wanted to look like a family-values poster. Then they'd ship me off somewhere so I wouldn't get in the way of their lives. I didn't really know them very well. And still don't," she added, regret in her tone.

"You were a neglected kid, too?" He'd never realized that something as fundamental as parental love was lacking in her life almost as much as in his.

"I was starved for affection, but my childhood hardly compares with yours. Thank goodness I had Stella and Homer to show me what a home could be like."

"Me, too," he said, recalling his own unstable existence, his tone gruff with emotion that he managed to suppress.

"Aunt Stella encouraged me to read, not just because it's educational, but because she knew I was shy and something of a misfit at school. I'll always be grateful to her for the freedom and adventures I found in books."

"Is that why you teach first-graders, to help them learn to read?"

Her face brightened. "Yes. And that's why I want to teach adults to read, as well."

But not enough to put her own money into the venture, he recalled.

"I've bared my soul, so now it's your turn. You told me about the bicycle, but what else?"

"Stella and Homer insisted I was as good as anyone else, even though I didn't believe it for a long time. They taught me that character counts, not appearances, not money. They worked to build a sense of responsibility in me."

He couldn't tell her, but he especially remembered Homer's wise counseling when, at age eighteen and awash in hormones, Wade developed the hots for her.

"Men have got a problem, son. I call it testosterone poisoning, and medical science hasn't come up with a cure for it. You got to learn self control."

Homer made sure that his grandnephew spent the summer chopping firewood, even though they had no fireplace, and building a henhouse, in case they ever decided to go into the egg business. The old man had made sure Wade exhausted his body, burning up frustrations in the process.

But it was more than heat and hormones that plagued him. Laurel was pale and pure and perfect at fifteen. He fantasized about stealing her away from the world and keeping her as his own, knowing all the while that she'd never be his.

But still he'd fantasized.

"I remember when I was sixteen," he said, grasping at a less revelatory memory, "and you followed me around, showing off and imitating my bad habits."

"Actually I had a case of hero worship."

"Who was your hero?" He kicked himself for asking, expecting her to name some Ivy Leaguer in training.

"You, of course."

"Me?" He'd have been less startled if she'd said Charles Manson. He cut her a glance to gauge her attitude, and she smiled wryly.

"Sure. You were older—a man, I thought. You smoked cigarettes and wore the pack rolled up in the sleeve of your T-shirt. You ditched school. Cursed a lot. Had a mean reputation. You were my father's nightmare incarnate. So of course I thought you were the coolest thing since the training bra."

"You had high standards for a hero. I hate to break your heart, but I thought you were as pesky as a swarm of gnats."

"I remember. So I decided to learn to smoke to impress you. I'm sure I looked very mature with a cigarette dangling from my thirteen-year-old mouth."

"You didn't impress Homer. He urged me to quit smoking as an example for you."

"Did you?" she asked expectantly.

"Not until two years later. I didn't want anyone to think I'd done *anything* for you."

"You grabbed a cigarette from my hand, threw it away and promised to spank me if you caught me smoking again. I thought you were being mean, as usual. But that was my last cigarette, and I should have thanked you for that."

"Better late than never." So she'd had a crush on him at thirteen. Too bad she'd outgrown it so easily, he thought wryly.

She favored him with a smile that warmed him down to his toes. "You felt responsible for me!" Her pleased smile turned into one of smug satisfaction. "Wade Taggart, the baddest dude in town, was looking out for me."

"Yeah, but don't tell anybody. You'd ruin my reputation."

Chapter Eight

A few minutes later Stella awoke from her nap, stretched languorously, lit a cigarette and watched the road. "There!" she shouted suddenly. "Turn left right now."

Wade's swift reaction amazed Laurel, for he managed to swerve onto the narrow, pothole-ridden road despite the lack of notice. After a mile or so, the pavement ended, replaced by two narrow, twisting ruts, no more than a trail. The cars ahead of them churned up thick clouds of fine, white dust.

"Isn't this exciting?" Stella chirped. "I feel like a pioneer moving west."

Struggling to breathe without choking, Laurel rolled up her window, as did Wade. That helped, but the car was in such bad condition that dust penetrated around the windows and doors and even curled up from leaks in the floorboards, swirling around the urn clamped between her feet.

"Oh, that's better," Laurel lied, determined to be pleasant for Stella's sake. She put her hand over her mouth and nose in a futile effort to filter out the dust. "How long will it take to get to the canyon?" she gasped.

"It's twenty-six miles, dear."

On this road, twenty-six miles might as well have been a thousand!

"Wet down handkerchiefs for yourself and Stell, Princess, and spread them over your nose and mouth. That will keep out some of the dust."

"I don't need one, dear. It will interfere with my smoking." Stella lit a cigarette and blew a cloud toward the front seat. Laurel held a moist handkerchief to her dust-coated face and offered the other to Wade, but he declined.

"I've got to keep both hands on the wheel," he gasped. As he spoke, the rutted road turned into a washboard, a continuous series of uneven rows, slanting to the right and tugging the car toward the steep ditch.

"Watch out, Wade!" Laurel shouted louder than she'd intended.

He cursed softly, his jaw tightening as he wrestled with the steering wheel. "Thanks for the sound advice, Princess."

"I thought we were going off the road," she explained crossly.

"And that I wouldn't notice?"

"I've had as much fun as I can from sitting beside a disabled car."

"And I haven't?" he snapped.

"The Anasazi were an ancient people," Stella piped up as though neither of them had spoken, "the forerunners of modern Native Americans. They also built the cliff dwellings at Mesa Verde in Colorado. Most remarkable.''

Wonderful! A history lesson, Laurel thought sourly while sipping water to clear her throat of dust and smoke, with very limited success.

"Have you noticed," he muttered, "that the temperature in here is close to the boiling point? Or are you too busy minding my driving?" He rolled his window down partway.

More dust poured in, but the air was slightly cooler. Half a mile down the road a car maneuvered carefully toward them, sliding sideways.

"Wade!" she warned.

"I see them," he snapped, edging toward the side of the road to give the approaching car as much space as possible. "Do you want to drive?"

Drive this old heap on what could barely be called a road? No way. "Sorry. I didn't mean to criticize," she grumbled.

"Yeah. Okay."

As they made slow, tortuous progress toward their destination, Stella continued her monologue as though oblivious to the tension in the front seat, seemingly impervious to the dust and heat—and to the cigarette smoke she continued to generate. "The Anasazi were traders, and they built roads in the eleventh century that can still be seen today."

"This is probably one of them," Wade growled, jerking the wheel to avoid a pothole the size of a crater.

Despite her best efforts to stay angry, Laurel laughed, then regretted it when she coughed on the intake of dust.

At last they reached a well-paved portion of the road. They arrived at the park, paid their admissions, received a copy of the park rules and entered the site of the ancient civilization. Wade stopped the car beside a ruined building, its walls constructed of stones that had been shaped by hand and set in place a thousand years ago.

"Amazing," Laurel said, opening her door, eager to explore now that she could breathe freely again.

"No, dear, this isn't the right place," Stella said.

Wade waited until Laurel closed the door again, then drove slowly for a few minutes.

"Here! Stop right here."

He slammed on the brakes, ground to a halt and looked around. "There's nothing here, Stell."

"Look over there, dear," she said patiently, pointing to the right. "In the distance. There's a lovely old building there."

"That place is half a mile from here, and there's no road."

"We'll walk."

"No, Stell. The terrain is too rough. I'm not sure I could make it in this heat. Princess definitely couldn't."

Laurel bit her tongue to keep from accepting Wade's implied challenge and marching to and from the ruin. It wasn't her welfare that concerned Wade. He knew the distance was too great for Stella but didn't want to make her sound infirm.

His tact and concern touched Laurel's heart. Once again she wished he would care for her, look out for her as he had when he was sixteen. It seemed unlikely, though, given that they had only a tenuous agreement to pretend to be friends for Stella's sake—an agreement they'd breached less than a day after they'd made it.

"Laurel, get out of the car and take the urn with you!" Stella said petulantly. "This was an important place for Homer and me."

Laurel reviewed the park rules, relieved to find an out. "We can't go over there, Aunt Stella. But we can explore the ruins that are close to the road."

"I don't care what those silly rules say. Homer and I went there. It was lovely. Now get out of the car!"

Hot, sweating, her lungs still burning from the dust she'd inhaled, Laurel's temper was close to exploding. *You owe this woman more than you can ever repay. She loves you more than anyone in the world. She's not herself this morning. Be patient,* she ordered herself.

"No, Aunt Stella," she said as gently as she could manage. "We can't do what you want. I'm sorry."

"Wade?" she implored.

"No, Stell," he said firmly. "Let's go to the park office. It'll be cool inside. I bet they have information about the Anasazi we can study while we rest."

"Harrumph! Hand me that urn, Laurel." She snatched the container, dumped a small pile of ashes into her hand and flung them through Wade's open window, apparently not caring that most of them blew back on him.

Laurel stifled a laugh at Wade's startled expression, wondering what he would do to remove the fine layer of his great-uncle's remains that clung to his face, beard and hair, without seeming disrespectful to the deceased.

"Let's put the urn away now, Stell," he said evenly, making no move to brush away the ashes. "Then we'll go to the information center and cool off."

"No," she said, her chin jutting defiantly. "We're leaving. You two have absolutely no sense of fun and adventure."

"Would you like to take a couple of pictures?" Laurel asked, making sure her tone was placating. "Wade and I will pose by one of the ruins for you."

"I don't want pictures of just any old broken-down building. I have dozens at home. Let's go. You two are dull and boring," she carped just loud enough to be heard, and without much conviction in her tone.

When Wade started the car, Laurel didn't know whether to be relieved or disheartened about their departure. Their quarrel seemed to be over, and they'd cooperated for Stella's benefit, but they still had to navigate twenty-six miles of miserable road. As they slogged through the heat and dust, she decided to make an offer of peace to Wade.

She dampened a handkerchief with cold water from the ice chest. Leaning closer to him, she was all too aware of his long, bare legs and the powerful shoulder and upper arm she couldn't avoid brushing against. Holding her breath, she wiped his face with the wet cloth, swiping away caked dirt and Uncle Homer's ashes from his face and beard, leaving cool dampness in their place.

He glanced at her appreciatively, as though she'd performed lifesaving surgery on him. Taking one hand from the steering wheel, he lifted her fingers to his lips and kissed them gently. "I shouldn't have lost my temper, Laurel. I'm sorry."

"It was my fault, too," she said, curling her hand into his when he started to withdraw, her breathy tone betraying the effects of his soft lips and crisp beard on her skin. "We promised to be friends."

Stella's approving sigh wafted from the back seat, borne on a cloud of cigarette smoke.

Exhausted but unable to sleep that night, Laurel left the bed, moving carefully so Stella wouldn't wake up, went to the dirt-streaked window of the motel room and stared out at the gravel parking lot.

A few minutes later a furtive movement caught her eye. A man—no two men. Intrigued, she watched them creep between cars. They stopped and looked around. In the weak light a moment passed before she realized they'd stopped by Stella's car.

Anger rose up in her. Those jerks were messing with the wrong car! She darted for the door, opening it quietly and leaving it ajar behind her.

"Hey!" she called out in the near dark, running barefoot down the rusting metal stairs. "Hey! What the heck do you think you're doing?"

The men turned in unison, froze for an instant, then ran.

"Come back here, you creeps!" she shouted. "You won't get away with that!"

The men dashed out of the lot and around the corner. Without thinking, she ran after them, stopping after a few agonizing steps as sharp gravel bit into her bare soles.

"Laurel, what is going on?" Wade caught her from behind, swung her into his arms and strode behind the shelter of the staircase.

Flustered at this turn of events, at the strength of his arms wrapped around her back and beneath her knees, at the powerful planes of his bare chest beneath her palms, she shouted, "Put me down! Dammit, Wade. Let me go."

Lights flicked on in several rooms, and a couple of doors scraped open upstairs. An angry male voice demanded an explanation.

"Everything's okay," Wade shouted, as he slid her down the length of his body until her feet touched the ground. He held her against him loosely, and she made no effort to move away, dimly wondering why.

"Oh, yeah?" A pair of booted feet stomped down the stairs.

"Say something, for God's sake, Laurel," he whispered harshly. "I don't want this guy to beat me up for saving you from yourself."

Suddenly frightened by her own stupidity, she clung weakly to Wade, pressing her fingers against his chest, seeking his strength, his protection. "I'm all right," she forced the words past the knot wedged in her throat.

"You've got to do better than that." He set her away from him, keeping his hand on her upper arm.

She peered at the huge stranger barreling up behind Wade. "Uh, thanks, but I'm all right. Really."

When the man halted, looking unconvinced, she added, "I thought someone was stealing my aunt's car, that's all. They're gone."

"You know this man?" he asked gruffly, indicating Wade with a jerk of his thumb.

"Yes. Thank you," she said, her voice stronger now. The man shrugged and strode up the stairs.

"Jeez, Princess. You got a death wish? You're courageous— I'll give you that. But did you really think anyone would steal that wreck of a car? It's not worth the trouble of hauling it off."

"I...I thought they were stealing from Aunt Stella," she said defensively. "I wasn't going to let them have anything of hers." A little calmer now, she added, "I didn't think, I guess."

He dropped his hand from her arm, taking his warmth from her. "I admire your spunk, but your judgment could use some improvement." He took a backward step and let his gaze rove over her, then lifted an eyebrow. "I also admire that transparent night-gown, Princess."

She looked down at her gown. Backlit by the light above a door, she might as well have been naked. Fighting the urge to cover the strategic parts of her anatomy with her arms, she marched up the stairs to her room with the little dignity she could muster, fully conscious that Wade followed, treating himself to a view of her backside.

Her frustrations compounded when she found the door to her room had swung closed and locked. "No! Oh, no!" she said in a harsh whisper. She'd either have to cause another commotion to wake Stella, who slept like a rock, or wake up the motel manager and ask him for another key. In a seminaked state.

"Need some help?" Wade leaned against the wall, arms crossed over his moonlight-kissed chest, and watched as she stomped her bare foot, then bit back a curse when it made contact with the rough concrete.

Indignant at his insolence, his near nudity, and her pulse-pounding response, she stretched to her full height and said in what she hoped was an imperious tone. "Yes. Go see if you can get me another key."

"Aw, the old guy needs his sleep." He pulled his own room key from the front pocket of his low-slung cut-offs. "You can stay with me, Princess," he teased. "I won't bite."

"I'm not afraid of being bitten," she snapped.

"Then what are you afraid of?"

You! Me! her brain shouted in alarm. "I'm not afraid of anything," she said stoutly and discovered that something had gone wrong with her breathing.

"Lightning's going to strike you for telling such a huge lie, Princess. But come inside. I need you." He unlocked his door and held it open for her. His taunting grin dared her to refuse.

She wanted to be with Wade more than she cared to contemplate. To be enfolded in his arms again. To be needed by the only man who could send her up in flames without really trying. The man she was falling in love with, despite her strongest efforts to avoid it.

In love? Instinctively she sought to deny it. She couldn't possibly be falling for Wade Taggart.

Yes she could, she admitted. Blast!

"I . . . I . . ." *I used to be fairly articulate,* she chided herself. "All right," she said softly, aware she was throwing caution to the winds and not caring.

He followed her into the small room that seemed to shrink as he entered. He glanced around the cramped space, hastily grabbed a pile of papers from the bed and stuffed them into the top dresser drawer.

As he swept the faded brown spread from the bed and draped it around her shoulders, she wondered idly what he'd been doing when she'd sounded the alarm a few minutes ago. What were those papers all about? She didn't care, for he was standing inches from her in the dim lamplight.

Trouble! Danger! Run for your life! her brain shrieked. Her body defied the order. She raised her hand and placed it on his chest, the contact with his firm, bare skin and crisp, black hair sending fizzing excitement—*anticipation*—through her warming body.

She loved Wade Taggart, couldn't imagine loving another man like this. But, she reminded herself sternly, he had no interest in marriage. At least he'd been honest about that. She shouldn't settle for a short-term affair, knowing that he wanted her in a physical sense but would never love her.

She had to get away while she still could, for if he kissed her, she'd likely lose her resolve. Prying her hand off his chest, she said, "I'd better go to my own room. I'll call Aunt Stella from here and ask her to open the door."

"Don't go. I said I need you."

"I don't think so," she said, fighting the urge to capitulate. "It's not a good idea for me to... to, uh..."

"Remove my stitches?" Mischief danced in his eyes.

"Stitches? What?" Then she understood. He was *toying* with her, pretending he wanted her to make love, but all he really wanted was someone to tend to his stupid wound!

"Do I look like your personal nurse, Wade?" She aimed for a sarcastic tone, but got one edged with disappointment, tinged with bitterness.

He ran his gaze over her slowly, as though considering her question. "Not at the moment, now that you mention it. But it's time to get them out, and I haven't seen a clinic since we left Amarillo. Come on, be a sport. I borrowed Stella's manicure scissors, tweezers and a couple of alcohol swabs. I tried to take them out myself, but I can't manipulate the surgical instruments by looking in the mirror. I keep stabbing myself."

She should be pleased at this turn of events. Ripping sutures out of his head was certainly safer than kissing him. Or making love to him.

But, romantic fool that she was, she'd always expected that the realization she was in love would involve a tender moment with the object of her love, a quiet time to reflect on their relationship, their future.

But she and Wade hardly had a relationship, much less a future.

"Okay," she said, pushing a smile into place. "Just call me Florence Nightingale." She followed him into the minuscule bathroom, tore open an alcohol swab and prepared to disinfect the nearly healed scar. *Too close.* She couldn't avoid pressing against him as she reached up to his scalp with unsteady hands. "This won't work," she said on a shaky breath.

"Works fine for me," he teased, wrapping an arm around her back and pulling her closer for a moment, then releasing her.

She backed out of the bathroom still clutching the swab. "Out here is saf—better." Sinking onto a corner of the bed, she pulled a pillow into her lap and cleared her throat. "Here," she ordered.

Obligingly, he handed her the tweezers and scissors, lay on the edge of the bed and rested his head on the pillow, his nose mere inches from her belly button. This arrangement was *not* safer, but if she insisted that he change positions, he'd only tease her, make her more uncomfortable.

She drew a breath intended to soothe her edgy nerves. It failed miserably, leaving her with a pair of sharp scissors in unsteady hands. After cleaning the instruments with alcohol, she carefully cut the first suture then tweezed it from the head of her own true love.

Ah, romance.

Memories of the night when he'd been hurt flooded her mind. How he'd sheltered her against the violence

surrounding them, how her pulse had jumped erratically as he'd turned his back on danger, making himself an easy target. How she'd wanted to put her arms
around him and kiss the daylights out of him even
though she'd actively disliked him then.

She finished her task and sighed in relief. "Okay,
Wade. Get up." *So I can work at breathing normally
again,* she added to herself.

He planted a quick kiss on her tummy and rolled to
his feet, apparently unaware of the heat and breath-
lessness he'd generated in her. Again. She stood and
moved to the phone, preparing to escape his over-
whelming presence.

"You promised to stay." His teasing wink dared her
to refuse. "I won't touch you, wouldn't even think
about it. In fact, I'll sleep on the floor like a Boy Scout
would."

It was all a joke to him, she thought. He'd led her
on, got her to minister to his injury, but otherwise had
no use for her.

He took the bedspread from her shoulders, dropped
it on the ratty carpet and tossed a pillow on top. "Get
in the bed."

She lay down on the sagging mattress, wondering if
he'd keep his promise, half hoping he wouldn't. He
tucked the faded sheet around her, then kissed her, a
gentle, fleeting kiss that left her wanting more . . . and
cursing herself for her weakness.

"Good night, Laurel. Sleep well."

"I will, but you won't. The floor is too hard."

"No harder than I am." His sexy grin played over his
lips for a moment before he turned off the light and,
guided by the pale moonlight, settled onto his makeshift pallet.

As she tried to relax and go to sleep, she worked at convincing herself it was for the best that Wade didn't love her, didn't even need her. Her life was too conventional for a man like Wade to share. He wouldn't settle down as husband to a simple school teacher. Even if she managed to convince him to give it a try, boredom was bound to drive him away after a while.

If she were willing to accept a semipermanent relationship—which she wasn't—she could picture the reaction of her conservative school board whenever Wade blew into Edgarville—shaggy, unshaven, ill clothed and driving a wreck of a car. Ms. Covington's "guest" would be the talk of the town, the cause of whispers and raised eyebrows.

Nor could she traipse around the country with him, drifting from job to job. She'd never be comfortable with that kind of life, even though she'd be with Wade. She'd invested too much of herself in her career and in the literacy center. She couldn't give them up in a futile attempt to make him happy.

She didn't even know what he wanted out of life, except to be footloose and fancy-free.

"Who are you, Wade? Really," she asked tentatively.

"Not your Mr. Comfortable, Princess. Not even close." He sounded no more content than she was.

Loud knocking dragged Wade into semiconsciousness, and he struggled to gain his bearings.

"Wade, wake up!" Stella's voice urged from outside his door. "Laurel's missing!"

Last night's events invaded his brain.

Laurel! He turned his head toward the bed, wincing at the stiffness in his neck. She was sitting up, blinking slowly and sleepily pushing her hair away from her face.

"Oh, Lord!" she whispered, startled at their being discovered.

He stumbled to the door, opened it and staggered when sunlight struck his eyes.

"Wade! She's gone! We have to find her!" Stella looked past him and took in the scene. "Ohhh..." she said knowingly, her gaze fixed on Laurel's dishabille.

She stepped into the room, her gaze flicking from the pallet on the floor to the unmussed half of the bed. "Ohhh," she said, disappointment in her tone.

Wade hadn't blushed in fifteen years, had forgotten the way heat surged to his face. His cheeks burned now as though he'd been caught in the midst of some perverted act.

Laurel scrambled from the bed, snatched up the bedspread and covered herself. She lurched toward the door, grabbed the room key from Stella's hand and dashed into her room.

"My, my, my." Stella surveyed the room more carefully, her gaze pausing on the open snap at the top of his cutoffs. "Did you two have a good time last night, dear?" she asked hopefully.

"Uhh..." How could he respond to a question like that? Holding Laurel, touching her sweet body had brought him to the brink of desire. But he'd known that nothing lasting could come of it, that she was not the woman who'd make a home for him, to share his life forever. Those simple facts had left him determined to protect her.

Even from himself. So he'd played it light, pretending he only wanted her help removing his sutures. Pretending he wanted nothing more with her.

"It's a simple question, dear," Stella prompted

"She chased two possible thieves away from the car but locked herself out of your room," he said, skirting the issue.

"She did? She's valiant, isn't she, risking her life to protect my little car? Just the kind of woman you need, Wade."

Need, but never will have.

He couldn't bear to analyze his feelings in the presence of his hopeful aunt. "You two pack up and go have breakfast at the café. I'll be there in a minute."

"All right." Stella yanked her camera from her purse and snapped his picture.

Jeez, she could blackmail him with that shot.

He closed the door, welcoming the gloomy silence and called his office.

"How's it going, chief?" Marla asked.

"Well enough, I guess." He recounted the misadventure at Chaco Canyon.

"How are you and the princess getting along?" Marla teased.

"I don't really know," he said on a weary sigh. "One minute everything's fine, the next..." *One minute I want to make love to her, the next I'm scared of loving her.* "She's driving me nuts."

"Keeps you awake at night?"

"Oh, yeah." He sighed again, long and slow, recalling his nearly sleepless night on the floor with only a few feet of space between them.

After a moment of silence, Marla piped in a singsong voice, "Wade's got a girlfriend."

"If you weren't the only person in the world who knows where all my papers are filed, I'd fire your butt, Marla."

"I notice you didn't deny it." She paused as if waiting for him to respond, then continued. "Now that I'm terrified by the specter of unemployment," she mocked, "I'll relay the latest from Stavros. He and his London partner faxed me a bunch of changes their lawyers want in the draft agreement you sent. He wants you to analyze them, make sure there are no downsides he's missed. And he wants to hear from you ASAP."

"Yesterday I told him you'd make the changes and send them on to me," he said, relieved that he'd have something to work on today, something to keep his mind off Laurel.

"If there's a fax machine where you are, I'll send you their comments. But, Wade, they want you in Athens to close the deal."

"How soon?"

"In a week, maybe, according to Stavros. When will you be back in Dallas?"

"Despite the heat and car trouble, my aunt is hellbent on revisiting more 'special places,' but she still won't divulge how many or where."

A trip to Athens would save him from himself. And he had to be there to orchestrate the closing. After courting Stavros for a year, he wouldn't risk the deal cratering because significant details had been overlooked. He wanted to be in Athens, negotiating the final agreement.

But he couldn't leave yet. Wouldn't. For an instant he considered sending Marla to Greece as his liaison. But, well informed and reliable though she was, she wasn't qualified to make on-the-spot decisions for him. There was no one else he could send.

"If necessary, I'll have to stall Stavros. I can't leave the old girl or the princess in the middle of nowhere. Hold on and I'll check on a fax."

He located a list—a short one—of the motel's services and read Marla the number, then ended the call.

After breakfast à la Stella, he went to the office to check out and pick up the fax transmission. Laurel watched him fold the twenty pages and stuff them in his back pocket, her expression guarded. She asked no questions, and he fought the urge to explain what he was up to.

What could he say that would make a difference? He'd planted the idea that he had some sort of subsistence job, in order to protect himself, knowing she'd never be attracted—forever and always—to someone with no prospects and no concerns about his rootless existence.

He needed her to believe in that perception of him.

For the first time he asked himself why.

Chapter Nine

Wade stowed their luggage in the trunk and crawled behind the steering wheel, ignoring Laurel's puzzled expression. "Where to, Stell?" he asked, when he got the car started.

"The Four Corners, of course," she said as though any fool would have known. Consulting the map, she read off highway numbers.

As he drove, he glanced at Laurel from time to time. When their gazes collided, electricity pulsed between them for that instant. Then she turned her head, breaking eye contact, her face flushing.

He was relieved, he told himself, that she wanted to distance herself. He didn't want to be the only one who felt vulnerable in the morning's bright light.

He glanced her way again and found her studying him, felt the same tension for an instant, until she lowered her lashes to conceal her eyes. He wanted to talk with her, was tempted to tease her about her electric blue outfit with two red sequin lips clinging to her breasts. The words stuck in his throat. He was in no mood to kid her about her clothes. Not after last night's odd intimacy had left him so unsettled.

Half an hour later they reached the place where New Mexico, Arizona, Utah and Colorado met. "Stop by the signpost, dear," Stella directed.

When Laurel retrieved the urn and stepped from the car, Stella climbed out without assistance, fairly dancing with anticipation.

She lifted the top from the urn and tipped a mound of ashes into her hand. Without a word, she hop-skipped around the sign, sprinkling Homer's remains in each of the four states. Grinning happily, she posed for pictures, then returned to the car.

"Homer always said this was the best place of all." Settled again in the back seat, she said, "Hand me the urn, Laurel, dear. I want to feel closer to my Homer for a while, to prolong the memory of our visit here."

What in the world could be special about this vacant place? Wade wondered. It was notable only because the borders of four states touched. That fact alone couldn't account for Stella's ebullience. He glanced at Laurel, but her expression was guarded, giving him no clue.

"Now, Wade, turn around and head west on this same road. Then hook a left at Highway 98, toward Page."

"To Grand Canyon?" Laurel asked, her tone enthusiastic.

"On the way back, perhaps. Homer and I did have a nice time when we river rafted through the canyon years ago. But," her eyes brightened as she spoke, "we're going to *Vegas!*"

"Vegas?" Wade was at a loss. "Why Vegas? You and Homer hardly seem the type to be attracted by gambling and glitz."

"It's very special to me," she said in a tone that brooked no further questions. So he shut up and drove. After a few miles, Stella yawned and handed the map to Laurel. "You take charge, dear. I'm going to catch a nap."

"How far is it to Vegas?" he asked his new navigator.

"At least four hundred miles," she said with a sigh. "Too far for a one-day trip."

"We need to make it in one day, even a very long one. We got an early start, thanks to our human alarm clock." He glanced in the rearview mirror. In repose Stella looked like a tired old woman. "She's pretty tough, but this trip is wearing her down. I want to get her off the road for a couple of days at a good hotel so she can rest comfortably."

"Good," she said somberly. "I've been worried about her since yesterday when she had that temper tantrum at Chaco Canyon. We were all in foul moods after that drive, but she didn't act like herself, tossing Homer's ashes out the window without caring where they landed."

An hour passed in companionable silence, punctuated by gentle snoring from the back seat. Laurel worked on lesson plans, which kept their gazes from meeting.

He had work to do, as well. He needed to review Stavros's comments on the agreement and fax a response, but he'd have no time until late tonight. He was already tired after getting so little sleep last night.

Memories of Laurel in his dreams, responding hungrily to his kisses, stole into his mind, hardening his body uncomfortably. He forced himself to think about Stavros's deal points instead.

It was that or drive across Arizona in a semiaroused state.

When she placed the envelope with her plans back under the urn and began watching the scenery, he asked, "Can you drive this car, Laurel? I need to take care of some stuff."

"I'll give it a try," she said warily.

He stopped the car, and they changed places, with his feet now cradling the urn. After a couple of false starts, Laurel got the car moving, and in a few minutes they were traveling smoothly—as smoothly as the rolling junk heap permitted. He should have figured that Laurel could drive an ancient car with recalcitrant standard transmission. She seemed able to do just about everything else, he thought sourly.

He pulled the faxed pages from his back pocket and began to read them, scribbling notes in the margin, shutting out the rest of the world. Hours later, he finished his work and realized he was hungry.

"Where are we, Princess?"

She frowned for a moment, then turned it into a smile that didn't engage her eyes. "We're close to Page and the Colorado River. There's a roadside park just ahead where we can have lunch. I didn't want to stop while you were working on . . ."

She paused, obviously waiting for him to complete the sentence. He wasn't about to enlighten her, so he said nothing.

After a long pause she continued. "Whatever. Stella's sleeping so well I hate to wake her, but she ought to eat."

He turned in his seat, scrupulously avoiding any contact with Laurel, and patted his aunt's hand until she opened her eyes and gave him a sleepy smile. They set out their picnic on a wooden table at a roadside park and ate their peanut butter sandwiches in the scanty shade provided by a grove of piñon trees.

Reenergized, Stella regaled them with tales of past adventures in that area, including the time Homer killed a menacing rattlesnake near that very spot.

Laurel surreptitiously lifted her feet and curled her legs safely on the bench. He fought the urge to do likewise and surveyed the ground nearby with a careful eye.

"Stell, killing snakes, particularly deadly ones, holds little appeal for me. And I don't even want to think about snakebites."

"You're not the man Homer was, dear," she teased.

Not even close, he knew. Homer had been unafraid of loving, had made a commitment to Stella while he was a young man and kept it all his life.

Wade was afraid of trusting a woman, of falling in love with anyone, especially Laurel. No, he was afraid of *admitting* he loved her, afraid of telling her and facing the consequences.

Admitting he loved her? Where had that crazy thought come from? But he realized it was true, had been true since he was eighteen and awash in adolescent hormones. He'd been in love with her for nearly half his life.

Telling her was another matter. He had nothing to gain from speaking the truth. He'd adopted his ne'er-do-well persona to protect himself from her.

He'd succeeded too well.

"I'm ready to go gambling," Stella announced as she polished off her elaborate meal in the hotel's elegant restaurant late that night. "I'll go to the casino, but you two should go dancing."

Laurel shot a look at Wade, who seemed as reluctant as she was. All day she'd struggled to put aside thoughts of what had happened—and hadn't happened—last night, but with little success.

"Wouldn't you rather go to bed? It's been a long day," she suggested, hoping for a reprieve from Wade and from her own thoughts.

"No, dear. I hear a slot machine calling my name."

"There's one in our room you can use," she persisted.

"I like the noise and the lights and the crowd in the casino."

"Wouldn't you like to have company?" she asked.

"Why, no, dear. Gambling is a very private matter."

But should only be done in a crowd of strangers? She wanted to point out Stella's lapse in logic but realized it was pointless. Her aunt would go gambling by herself, period. "Will you stay in the hotel's casino and come straight to our room when you get tired?"

"Of course, dear. You can count on me to be careful," she said in her too-patient tone. "You two have a lovely time and tell me all about it in the morning." Her cherubic smile made Laurel wonder about its sincerity, but she capitulated. Stella strolled toward the casino, pausing to turn and wave at them.

"I'm not much of a dancer," Wade said as Stella departed. "Let's keep an eye on her for a while."

He moved with the grace of a jungle cat, so she doubted his disclaimer. But she didn't want to risk being in his arms, her body close to his, moving rhythmically together to soft music in dim, intimate light.

Correction. Her body clamored for all of that. Her brain warned of the danger, reminded her that Wade didn't want her, that disaster loomed. And her brain was winning. For now.

"Neither am I," she lied. "Besides, we're either stand-ins for a romantic evening she and Homer shared or—"

"We're being manipulated by a tireless matchmaker," Wade said, his face glum.

Together, but with a foot of space between them, they watched Stella play the slots and shared a secret smile when she whooped in excitement as the machine spilled out a few coins.

An hour later Stella spotted them, despite their efforts to blend in with the slot machines. "I'm going to bed, my dears, so you two can quit playing bodyguard and have some fun."

Wade caught Laurel's hand, keeping them a few paces behind their aunt. "She won't let you into the room for a while," he whispered, "because she's determined to keep us together." She knew he was right and didn't relish the scene Stella might make, given her recent mood swings.

He looked through the tall, wide windows where the brightly lit pool area stood out from the surrounding gloom. "Let's go outside and talk for a while."

Certain that he didn't want to talk about the history of gambling in America or some other safe subject, she agreed reluctantly. She was foolish to want to be with him while her emotions simmered in a vat of roiling hormones.

"Stella surprised me when she agreed to stay at this hotel and eat in the restaurant instead of insisting on a cheap motel and bad food," she ventured when they seated themselves in comfortable lounge chairs near the pool.

"Yeah," he agreed.

Waiting for him to say more, she ran a fingernail along the edge of the chair arm, then locked her hands together in her lap to conceal her edginess. "What did you want to talk about?"

"Stella."

"Oh." She released a pent-up breath, surprised at the frisson of disappointment that swept through her.

"She's determined to complete her mission, but we don't know where we're going."

"'That's part of the surprise, dear,'" she said, mimicking Stella's pronouncement at the start of the trip.

"She's got to have a better car. One with air-conditioning—something newer and roomier. Otherwise this trip will wear her down. She might get sick from the rotten conditions."

"I keep forgetting that she's seventy-five because she acts younger and livelier than me," Laurel offered, squirming at the thought that Wade might expect her to pay for a car for Stella. If necessary, she could manage small payments, but the money would have to come from funds she'd set aside for her literacy center.

But what about Wade? He did some kind of responsible work, she was sure of that after he began receiving faxes and apparently responded to them. But a man with a wardrobe of battered jeans and T-shirts and who owned a car no better than Stella's seemed unlikely to have much extra money, either, despite his earlier claim that he could afford to buy her a new car, but didn't want to hurt her feelings.

"A new car?"

"Or a good used one. I think she can afford it, but that doesn't matter."

"Oh?" *Here it comes.*

He leaned toward her and took one of her hands, the strength and warmth of him oddly reassuring. She studied his handsome face, the harsh light tingeing his dark hair with silver, emphasizing his high cheekbones and casting the planes of his face in shadow.

She was being absurd, admiring Wade's face, making herself all tingly inside, while discussing her aunt's automotive needs.

"She's given me so much over the years that I can't begin to repay," he said.

Except with a lifetime of your love and affection, she thought. For an instant she was jealous of Stella, jealous that her elderly aunt was the recipient of his tenderest feelings. Feelings she'd sell her soul to have bestowed on her.

Good Lord! She really was crazy in love.

"Me, too," she whispered past the lump of emotion that clogged her throat.

"I'm going to buy a car for her," he murmured.

"You are? But can you—?"

He placed his index finger gently across her lips. "Yes, I can afford it. Trust me."

"I do," she said softly. And for that moment, at least, she did.

The outdoor lights dimmed, enclosing the two of them in a warm cocoon. Dance music played softly through hidden speakers as the plump half moon slid slowly toward the horizon.

He stroked the back of her hand with his fingertips, sending now-familiar sensual thrills through her. Eyes closed, she let the romantic night, and Wade's touch, swamp her senses.

"Dance with me?"

"Hmm?" She withdrew slowly from her sensuous reverie to focus on his words. "Why? I thought you didn't dance."

"I can fake it in the near dark on a pool deck. And that's the only way I can wrap my arms around you without being pounced on by hotel security."

Oh, yeah! her body shouted. And for once her brain didn't protest. She stepped into his embrace and they began to dance, slowly circling the pool.

"I like the way you polish my belt buckle, little lady," he said, bringing to mind the cowboy in the Dallas bar. His big hands cupped her bottom, pulling her closer to him.

"For more effective polishing," he murmured into her ear.

"You didn't want me to dance with him."

"I was a jerk."

"Yes, but why?"

"I was jealous."

Surprised, she tipped her head back to search his face. "Why?"

"Because he could hold you and I couldn't."

She remembered how much she'd wanted to dance with Wade. "You could have."

"I was scared to death of touching you."

"You were? Why?"

"Because I knew this would happen." He bent his head and brushed his lips over hers, kissed the corners of her mouth lightly, then traced her lower lip with the tip of his tongue.

She opened to him, teased his tongue with hers, coaxing him, tempting him. His clean male scent was far more erotic than any cologne, his perfect body molded against hers, slowly swaying with the music.

He lifted his head, lips parted, his face taut with desire.

Desire for her.

He watched her, his dark eyes hooded, as his hands caressed her breasts. The tips peaked and throbbed under the slow, circling strokes of his thumbs, the thin fabric of her blouse creating light, erotic friction.

Clutching the hard muscles above his collarbone, she moaned as his tongue drove into her mouth again— deeper, faster.

More. Please, more.

Too soon, he lifted his head, breathed in shallow gasps that echoed hers and stared into her eyes.

Don't say you're sorry. Don't apologize. Don't walk away. Not tonight.

"Come to my room."

"Yes."

"You're sure?"

She nodded, certain now, despite all her reservations, that she wanted to make love with Wade, and consequences be damned.

He grasped her hand and strode rapidly into the hotel to the elevator bank. As they waited in the bright light, she felt as if Wade's hand prints were visible on her skin, as though passersby could take one look at her and know she'd been trying to climb Wade's body.

As the mirror-walled elevator whisked them toward their floor, she tried to avoid his hot, hungry gaze to gather her wits. But his face reflected back at her everywhere she looked.

Her body grew hotter and tighter under his multifaceted, passionate scrutiny. When the car stopped, they leapt out and raced down the hall. Sanity regained a tiny foothold in her brain.

Stella.

Cursing her overdeveloped sense of responsibility, she pulled on his arm and dug in her heels, slowing, then stopping him. He swung around and looked at her as though she'd lost her mind.

"I have to check on Stella."

"Yeah," he groaned, "you should." He swept her into a quick, hot kiss, then released her. "There's more where that came from, sweetheart. Hurry back."

"A quick peek." Entering the room on tiptoe, she opened the bathroom door a crack, turned on the light and moved to Stella's bed.

It was empty. She turned on a lamp. Stella wasn't there.

She dashed into the hall, caught Wade's sexy grin and returned it with a frown. "Stella's gone!"

"Let me look." Wade searched the room again, as though it had secret hiding places she'd overlooked, then reported their aunt's disappearance to hotel security. He scribbled a note and left it on Stella's bed, instructing her to contact security when she returned.

"Come on. We'll find her." He grabbed her hand and they raced toward the elevator. For an hour they searched every nook and cranny in the casino, restaurants, shops and parking lots, Laurel's heart pounding, her mind praying.

"We'll find her," he repeated, determination in his voice, his expression hard.

"Of course," she said, her voice breaking under the tension in her body.

He ground to a halt, his hands encircling her wrists. "We *will* find her, Laurel. She *will* be all right."

He looked so determined, so sure of himself that his words became promises, easing the panicky edge that rose higher in her each time they failed to find Stella.

Security called the police and the search widened. Wade and Laurel roared off in Stella's car, hoping to spot her on the streets. He wove in and out of traffic, his face a tense grimace.

He was afraid, she realized. As frightened as she was. "We *will* find her. She *will* be all right," she repeated his reassurances.

He shot her a grateful glance, and the semblance of a smile played at his lips. Then he returned to checking out people on the street, stopping occasionally to phone the police to ask about Stella.

Lord, she was glad he was here. He'd taken charge and organized their methodical search for Stella. Something about his manner, his stance, bespoke natural leadership. He took over and resolved their crises- *du jour*—the ash bust, Stella's injury, the car's breakdown, and every other scrape they got themselves into. She liked having someone else to share her burdens, to take charge sometimes. A man who could lead her, without dominating her.

Tonight he'd nearly led her to his bed, she mused. No, she'd been a full participant. Encouraged him with her fiery aggression. She'd never behaved so wantonly. Never so wanted to give herself to a man.

Except to Wade. But this time was different. Then, she'd been a teenager, exploring her sexuality, overwhelmed by her physical and emotional responses. Whereas tonight, she admitted wryly, she'd been a mature woman, exploring her sexuality, overwhelmed by her physical and emotional responses....

She'd willed herself to forget that she knew little about Wade. Where he lived. What he did for a living. Whether he could ever fall in love with her.

Only the last item mattered, she realized.

"I'm beat," Wade said as the orange and gray dawn broke over the desert. "Let's go back to the hotel, shower, have breakfast and start up again."

She agreed quickly, suddenly famished. As they rode the elevator, he slid his arm around her shoulders, holding her gently against him. She laid her head on the carved muscle of his chest and sighed out her exhaustion, fear and the pleasure of his comforting strength.

Minutes later she opened the door to her room and flipped on the light.

Stella lay in her bed, sound asleep, one leg in a cast elevated on pillows, a wheelchair at the ready.

"Holy—" Wade, said behind her. "Stell?"

Their aunt stirred, blinked against the light and moved to sit up.

"Lie still," Laurel insisted, gently pressing Stella's shoulders until she subsided again on the pillows. "We've been out looking for you," she said, pleased that her voice betrayed none of the panic that had gripped her. "What happened? Can you tell us?"

"Quit frowning and hovering, dear," she said, loud and clear. "I'm fine. I broke my foot while carrying out part of my mission."

"Spreading Uncle Homer's ashes? I could—" she glanced at Wade "—we could have gone with you."

"This was a very special place, dear. I wanted to go alone. I got some terrific pictures of the wonderful people who helped me at the casino, and the cab driver who took me to the hospital, and the lovely doctor who fixed me up. It was a wonderful adventure. Do you want to hear about it?"

"Of course we do," Wade assured her.

"Homer and I never stayed in Vegas. He was opposed to gambling because his father gambled a lot and often lost all his wages. But me, I'd always wanted to try my hand. I'm usually very lucky, you know."

"Uh-huh," Laurel agreed, wondering where this story would go.

"We stopped at a service station while passing through town. I slipped away to a sleazy casino and played the slots until Homer found me. He'd been frantic. We had our worst argument that night. Because of my deceit." She sat quietly for a moment.

Deceit? Laurel was the queen of deceit. She'd deliberately deceived Wade about herself. Then she'd fallen in love with him under false pretenses. How could she expect him to love the haughty woman she'd created? How could she change his perception at this late date?

She thought of telling him the truth about her finances and her current life-style, but she was wary of his reaction. He might pity her or mock her because she "only" had a teacher's salary to live on. Worse, he might conclude, correctly, that she'd been playing a game, that she couldn't be trusted. She wanted him to respect her, she realized, even though he didn't love her.

"Last night," Stella continued, "I found that old casino and sprinkled some of Homer's ashes around a slot machine. You see, I wanted to remind myself that not all of our time together was happy." She sniffled and wiped away a tear with her knuckle, her sorrow tugging at Laurel's heart.

"Each of us made mistakes, but we worked our way through the rough times because we couldn't bear to hurt each other."

Hurting each other was what she and Wade had done best for so many years. Since they'd agreed a few days ago to work together for Stella's sake, they'd bickered less. But they had a lifetime of hurting to overcome. Did Wade even want to try?

He bent over the bed and kissed Stella's forehead. "Let's all get some sleep, then we'll fly back to Austin as soon as we can."

"Oh, no," Stella protested stoutly. "We have to go to Bakersfield, California, and San Francisco, and I promised you the Grand Canyon, and—"

"Later, love." He touched a fingertip to her lips. "When you've recovered."

"Oh, Homer..."

"Homer would understand."

Straightening, he looked to Laurel for confirmation.

"Of course he would. We need to get you home for a while."

"You two are not much fun, you know," she said halfheartedly.

Wade headed for the door. "I'll check in with security and the police. Will you get us three first-class seats on the next flight to Austin?" He spoke diffidently, as though nothing important had almost happened between them tonight.

"First class?" she murmured. The cost would be horrendous, at least two thousand dollars. There wasn't that much room on her credit card, or in her checking account. She could write a check, then call her small, low-tech bank and hope they'd make a transfer from the savings account she'd earmarked for her literacy center.

"Stella and her cast will have to travel first class, and we need to be with her."

"Um . . . I'll . . . I'll take care of it."

He watched her for a moment, an odd look in his eyes. "Never mind. I'll handle it while I'm in the lobby."

"Let's get on with the napping," Stella ordered.

"I . . ." She struggled for a rational explanation for her reluctance. Another handy lie.

"No problem," he said and closed the door behind him.

Chapter Ten

"Put me down in the wheelchair, dear," Stella directed Wade as he carried her into her house that afternoon. "I need to make us a pitcher of lemonade."

"Into bed you go, Stell," he said firmly as he laid her down and arranged the pillows so her leg was elevated. "You won't be playing hostess for a few days, but I bet Laurel knows the recipe for lemonade. I'll get our luggage and pay the cab driver."

"I'm really all right, dear. I just broke one bone in my foot. There are twelve of them, you know, so one break hardly matters."

"One is enough," he said, suppressing a grin.

"Well, I don't want lemonade, anyway," she said crossly, weariness visible on her face, her movements slow. "My plans haven't worked out."

"I promise we'll visit the other special places when your foot heals."

"Not those plans, you young fool. Other plans. Important plans."

Matchmaking plans, he surmised. Those plans had been doomed from the start, and he didn't want to talk about them. "You sleep, and I'll go see if the princess needs help."

"I like it so much more when you call her Laurel. So does she."

So did he.

Tired but restless, not anxious to be alone with Laurel, he sat on the big, wooden porch swing, set it in motion with a shove of his foot and tried to relax in the cool, damp breeze that hinted at rain.

He'd let himself get entirely too close to Laurel Covington. He'd put his neck on the line every time he'd kissed her. Last night he'd nearly made love to her. Would have if Stella had stayed where she'd belonged.

Then what? He'd never been interested in no-strings one-night stands. His romantic relationships had always involved shared interests and values as much as the sharing of bodies. But a short-term affair was all he could expect with Laurel. Then she'd come to her senses and go back to her society boyfriend, her real life. And why not? He'd convinced her that he was semiemployed, footloose and a rotten prospect as a husband.

A far cry from the Mr. Comfortable she wanted.

There was another possibility. He could tell her the truth and try to change her perception of him. He considered shaving, getting a haircut, putting on better clothes and telling her what kind of man he really was. Maybe if he told her that he could provide her with all the material things she was used to, could pay for her literacy center if she chose—

He was kidding himself. He didn't want a woman—
not even Laurel—on those terms. He wanted a woman
who loved him, regardless of his past, his financial
condition or social standing. He needed a woman
who'd stand by him, help him become the kind of
husband and father he dreamed of being.

Laurel Covington, who'd walked away from her
marriage, was an unlikely candidate to be his wife. His
lover, maybe for a short time, but not his wife. It
wasn't enough. But... dammit, he was tempted.

His test was unfair, he knew, requiring her to accept
him at what she believed was his worst. But he couldn't
risk rejection. He had to know what kind of woman
she'd become, whether or not she'd stick with her man
through thick and thin.

Some things about her didn't add up, he acknowledged. When he asked her to charge the airline tickets,
she'd stiffened and her eyes had widened as though
he'd suggested she dance naked in the streets of Vegas.
Yet he knew she treasured Stella, would do anything in
her power for her aunt—except add a couple of thousand dollars to her credit card.

Could Ms. Laurel Covington be living beyond her
means? As a kid, she'd bragged about some sort of
trust fund. Perhaps she'd gotten control of the money
when she'd matured and had spent it unwisely. But she
didn't seem to be a big spender. In fact, she didn't seem
to be a spender at all. She hadn't bought anything on
the trip—not that they'd visited any shopping meccas.

She worked at a difficult job for a salary that would
be peanuts for a rich woman. She didn't talk about
noblesse oblige or make mere cash contributions to
salve her conscience. Laurel got in the trenches and did
the hard, and often thankless, job of helping others.

But what did he really know about her? He knew she could adapt to almost any situation when she wanted to, including making a sweltering trip for her great-aunt's sake. He knew she had a sense of humor and a comforting manner that put people at ease.

He knew her attitude toward him had changed during the trip. She'd listened when he'd spilled his guts about his childhood, had almost apologized for misjudging him. Had thanked him for looking out for her when she was a kid. Very unprincesslike behavior, he had to admit.

He knew she was capable of loving. She loved Stella, probably had loved her husband at some time, might even love that Lud guy she was involved with.

He wondered what difference any of this made. She didn't love him. She wanted him, but that knowledge had burned in him for twelve years. And wanting wasn't enough for him.

There was no point in torturing himself about what might have been. About a life that would never be.

His gloomy assessment was interrupted when Laurel, still wearing the fake leather skirt and iridescent yellow top that had served as her travel outfit, joined him on the porch. Hesitantly, without comment, she handed him one of the glasses of lemonade she held, then stood awkwardly as if looking for a place to sit.

He glanced around the porch for a chair, but there was none. He slid to one end of the swing and pointed to the other. "Take a load off, Princess."

The fine lines around her eyes deepened with tension at his words, but she murmured her thanks and sat at the far end.

The swing rocked back and forth, its rhythmic creak tweaking at his nerve endings.

Heavy, dark thunder clouds rolled in, laden with moisture from a tropical storm in the Gulf of Mexico and growling portents of a drought-quenching rain that would break the godawful heat.

Uneasy, downright irritable with the tensions within him, the electricity that thrummed between him and Laurel, and the heavy atmosphere, he wanted to clear the air. He wanted to shout his frustrations at her, demand explanations, make her as angry as he was.

Irrational.

He didn't care.

"I've been wondering, Princess," he said offhandedly, "why you asked me to kiss you way back when."

Laurel had avoided fully confronting that question for twelve years, had only let herself examine limited facets of that devastating encounter. She fought the urge to curl herself into a tight ball to protect against the sudden anger in Wade's face and voice.

She might as well spit out the truth, or at least a version of it. "I wanted to learn what sex was all about."

"Why me? You had plenty of Ivy Leaguers to choose from. The kind of men—hell, *boys*—your father approved of."

"That was the whole point," she said calmly, refusing to meet anger with anger. "You were safe. Word wouldn't get around school, unless I chose to tell. If I wasn't any good at sex, no one who mattered would know."

He drew back as though she'd struck him. "'*No one who mattered'?*" he growled. "So I was just some . . . sexual convenience for you to experiment with."

No! He'd been more to her than that! More than she'd admitted to herself. She'd wanted Wade Taggart, and no one else, to introduce her to sex, to make love to her. Even though she had been frightened by his potency, his raw strength.

She couldn't confess her true feelings after all those years. Not to this angry man who hadn't even wanted her when she'd needed him so much. She'd wanted him to love her, to fill that achingly empty part of her heart. That was why his cruel dismissal had hurt so much for so long... and still did.

No, she couldn't bare her soul at this late date. She looked him straight in the eye and lied. "Yes, an experiment."

He stood abruptly and strode to the end of the porch, pivoted and strode back. He stopped before her—tall, powerful, as likely to explode as the thunderheads swirling in the sky above them.

She didn't fear him, despite his strength. He had never hurt her—physically. The opposite was true. He'd made her safe from the dangers of smoking, the killing desert sun. From her own runaway emotions. She wanted to acknowledge his protection, but she didn't know what to say in the face of his anger.

He said nothing, watching the dark sky as fat raindrops fell forcefully, pelting the parched soil as minutes dragged by.

"Since it's truth or consequences time, Princess, you might as well know what I wanted out of that encounter." Grim-faced, he continued, "I wanted to dominate you, get even with you for being rich and pampered, everyone's little darling. I wanted to take your virginity because that was the one thing your daddy couldn't buy back for you."

"I'd have given it to you gladly. I was tired of being the only virgin in the junior class, and I felt...left out."

"You put a poor price on yourself, Princess, but I guess you knew your own worth."

"You took advantage of me to get revenge on my father and me. I didn't know what I was getting into. You should have—" *What? Stopped before anything dangerous happened? He had, but why?*

Steeling herself against the greater hurt that might come from knowing the truth, she asked, "Why did you stop when I was so...willing? You didn't have to humiliate me."

"If you haven't figured that out, Princess..." He scrubbed his hand down his weary face as if to wipe away the distasteful memory.

"We don't have to keep trying to hurt each other. There's no reason to." He walked to the front door and opened it, then paused and shot her a long, searching look.

"With luck we won't have to see each other for another twelve years. By then, maybe I'll be too old to care anymore."

"It's just as well, I guess." She heard her voice quaver and cleared her throat to disguise it. "We have nothing in common, do we? Except a great-aunt we both love. Except having used each other to make some point a long time ago."

He went inside, letting the screen door slap closed behind him as a thunder clap rattled the house.

Shaken by the storm raging around her and inside her, Laurel wrapped her arms around herself and stared at the brown rainwater rushing along the curb.

* * *

"There, dear, eat your breakfast," Stella urged Wade the next morning as he sat in a chair equidistant from Stella and Laurel. "Cereal and milk and toast and jelly were all I could manage from this darn wheelchair, but I'll be up and around in a few days, and I'll fix you a *real* breakfast."

"This is fine, Stell," he said, trying to sound jovial after another sleepless night. He poured a cup of coffee from the pot in front of him, took a sip and felt better as the well-flavored caffeine got his blood stirring sluggishly through his veins.

"Laurel made the coffee, dear. Isn't it good?"

"Best I've ever had," he said, forcing a smile but keeping his eyes off Little Miss Homemaker.

"Eat up, my dears," she said with her usual perkiness. "I've got a big day planned."

"Stell..." he said, reluctant to burst her bubble. "I've decided to go home today. I've got work to do, and I'm not needed here. The princess," he tilted his head in Laurel's direction but kept his gaze on his aunt, "can handle anything you need."

"Oh, no!" Stella set down her spoon and wailed. "You can't leave. I'm not finished with you yet."

"I know you had plans for the princess and me, Stell, but there's nothing between us." His throat seared from choking back his emotions.

"But I need you to help me scatter the last of Homer's ashes at the Zilker Park rose garden this morning. I've decided to end my quest with a visit to the most special place of all. You have to help with the wheelchair."

How could he refuse a request that would put an end to this foolish quest? After the visit to the park, he'd be on his way to Dallas. Then Athens. Then who knew where.

Or cared.

His verbal battle with Laurel had been stupid, fighting over a twelve-year-old kiss. But he knew now for certain that he'd never meant much to her. Still didn't, never would.

It was time to get on with his life.

"I'll get your parasol, Stell, and call a cab." He risked a look at Laurel, found her staring at him, her expression cold, her face drawn and pale with dark circles under her eyes.

He should have been pleased that she'd had a rotten night, but his heart went out to her. He wanted to hold her, comfort her, despite her curt dismissal of their relationship.

He loved her. He was a fool.

The ride to the park seemed interminable to Laurel. Last night's rain had brought merciful relief from the heat that had plagued Austin for three months, but the change in weather did little to dispel her sense of despair. Fortunately she could remain silent, because Stella told the driver all about her great adventures, including the one where Wade forged her name on the car title and gave her heap to a Vegas hotel bellman instead of a tip.

Laurel glanced at Wade through lowered lashes. He sat stone-faced in the back seat of the cab with her, huddled against his door as though he couldn't bear the thought of touching her. He probably couldn't.

She'd known she was risking her heart when she'd let herself open up with Wade. Until then, she'd been content with her false impressions about him as a child.

She'd accepted his insult about her womanliness as his true opinion. But he had turned out to be an admirable man in many ways, and she'd let herself care about him. Worse, she'd let down her guard and fallen in love with him.

Unable to carry on even a semblance of conversation, she lagged behind Wade as he pushed Stella's chair along winding paths between elevated gardens made of white limestone and holding clusters of flower-laden rosebushes.

"They were pink. I'm certain of that. Do you see them yet, dear?" Stella asked Wade. "Oh, over there, by the edge of the garden, just this side of the trees. That's the one."

He pushed the wheelchair completely around the rose bed while Stella studied it, making sure it was indeed the right one. Satisfied, she directed him to the side of the bed nearest the trees, opened the urn and set free Homer's ashes on the slight breeze. She sat still for a minute, her wistful smile gradually becoming a grin.

"Okay, Stell," Wade said, "it's time to tell us about the ashes. Why did you have to scatter them at those particular places?"

"You two just don't get it, do you? You haven't figured out what I've been up to," she said with a tender, reminiscent smile. "You see, I've been spreading Homer's ashes at all the places where we made particularly spectacular love."

"Aunt Stella?" she said, startled by her aunt's boldness. "The dark passageway at the fairgrounds?"

She shrugged eloquently. "Our first quickie."

Her aunt and uncle had quickies? Good Lord.

"That car hulk at Cadillac Ranch?" Wade asked, a smile playing at his lips when she nodded. "The Four Corners?"

"All four states, dear. Homer was prodigious."

Her kindly great uncle had been a prodigious lover?

Wade laughed out loud, a rich, happy sound. Infectious, Laurel admitted, releasing the laugh she'd been too surprised to let go. She wondered what his eyes looked like when filled with humor. Those gold flecks must be dancing mischievously in his black irises, she decided, but his sunglasses concealed them when she dared to cast a glance at him.

"Those are great memories, Stell. A tour of all the places where your hormones erupted."

"Not all the places. Just the best ones," she corrected in the tone of a teacher whose student misstated significant facts. "And it wasn't just sexual urges . . . it was love at its very best."

"It's too bad we didn't create some spectacular memories of our own," he said to Laurel, his smile wilting.

"But you did," Stella insisted as she whipped out a handful of pictures and began passing them around. "We almost got arrested for transporting Homer's ashes, shared a pickup with those dreadful chickens, survived the trip to Chaco Canyon. And you searched all over Vegas for me. Where else could we have such great fun?

"And look here. You two got to know each other better," she continued, handing a photo to her niece.

Laurel stared at the picture of her and Wade kissing in the back of the pickup with his shirt draped over her head, her nose reddened from allergies and sunburn, her expression blissful.

Oh, yeah, they'd gotten to know each other better. She'd fallen in love with Wade Taggart. Even without pictorial evidence, she'd treasure those memories though they'd always be tinged with the pain of his disinterest in her for anything—except, possibly, sex.

To conceal the tears she feared would spill over her eyelids, she strolled closer to the roses, tugged on a stem to bring an opening bud to her nose and sniffed its sweet, heady aroma.

Not a good move, she decided, letting go of the flower. Roses reminded her of weddings.

"Now, my dears, I do have one little confession to make. I brought you along because I thought you'd fall in love if you had enough time—and a little push. I figured if the circumstances were bad enough, you'd cooperate together against the elements—and your crazy old aunt. So I bought that wretched car with no air-conditioning, and I smoked and smoked and smoked. I may never get that nasty taste out of my mouth. And those horrible meals. I thought surely you'd revolt, but no."

"When you fell and tore my dress?"

"I hadn't expected the ground to be quite so hard, but that dress had to go. And my knees are nearly healed."

Laurel quelled a shudder. Stella's matchmaking efforts had surpassed all they had surmised. She'd endangered her own health to bring them together. And all for nothing.

Stella forged ahead despite the heavy silence from her listeners. "I pretended to take long naps so you could talk privately together. Do you have any idea how hard it is to snore on purpose for hours on end? And still nothing happened.

"In desperation, Laurel, dear, I even locked you out of our room the night you ran to save my car." She let loose a gusty sigh. "Nothing happened then, either."

She fixed Laurel, then Wade, with a misty-eyed smile. "I failed, but I learned a good lesson, and I won't interfere with your lives again." With her index finger, she sketched an X on her chest. "Cross my heart," she said contritely, then paused to wait for their reactions.

Laurel wanted to assure her, albeit falsely, that no harm had come from her misguided efforts, but she couldn't force the words past the lump in her throat.

"Now, my dears, I had so hoped that you'd fall in love, and I wanted to share a special moment with you right here. This is where Homer and I spoke our own made up marriage vows more than fifty years ago. We did it privately, without a minister or judge or friends."

"A common law marriage?" Wade asked in obvious surprise.

"Technically. But, of course, there was nothing *common* about it. We promised to love each other till death do us part, and we did, even though we had our share of problems. We said the words right where you are standing, Laurel."

Feeling like she'd trampled on sacred ground, Laurel scuttled sideways.

"I hoped the two of you, the people I love most in the world, would want to say your own vows at this special place. But since you're not getting along, I'll just have to live with only my fading memory. Which I'll treasure for the rest of my life. Of course, I don't have many years left, so it doesn't matter."

No! Laurel's mind screamed. *Don't volunteer.* She was no masochist, wanting more pain added to her burden, repeating solemn but empty vows with a man who didn't love her, just to give her aunt a fresh memory. She tensed, waiting for Wade's derisive comment. Something about hell freezing over, she expected.

She knew her aunt was manipulating them again, despite the promise that had just fallen from her lips. Stella was trying to force a pledge of love that didn't exist for one of them. She drew a long breath, expelled it slowly, then ventured a look at him. He was watching her, his face impassive.

"Ah, well, my dears, it's all right. Really," Stella murmured. A lone tear trickled down her cheek, melting Laurel's resolve because this place, those memories, were particularly poignant for her aunt.

She could go through this pretense for Stella. She could survive nearly any pain that lasted only a few minutes because it meant so much to the woman who'd given her so much love for all her life.

But what about Wade?

He doesn't know you love him, her mind nitpicked. *You've never revealed your true feelings.* A tiny spark of hope ignited. Maybe, if he knew how she felt, understood why she'd pretended to be someone she no longer was—had never been . . .

He had a right to know he was loved, even if it was a love he didn't return. He'd admitted that no one, except for his aunt and uncle, had ever loved him. Perhaps, if nothing else, he'd find reassurance in knowing he was easy to love. Someday he might find a woman who'd fill his needs, and he'd risk loving her.

Her heart was breaking anyway, she thought grimly. Her own fear of rejection and humiliation paled beside her sudden, urgent need to tell him the truth about her feelings for him.

Sniffling softly, Stella wiped her eyes with a handkerchief.

Laurel drew another long breath, struggling to rein in her galloping pulse, to keep her voice level. "I have to talk with Wade first. In private."

His face solemn, he tilted his head toward the clustered trees, then walked toward them. She followed on leaden feet, searching for the right words. When he stopped in a shady area and pulled off his sunglasses, she leaned against a tree trunk, unwilling to trust her legs to support her. He stood three feet away, looking wary, but saying nothing.

"I have to tell you some things about me. Things you should know." The twin grooves around his mouth deepened as though he was bracing himself for bad news.

"About my money...my so-called fortune—"

"It's long gone, isn't it?" He spoke softly, without the jeering tone she'd anticipated her admission would bring.

"Yes. Phil, my ex-husband, embezzled from my father's company and from me. When he had most of the money, he took off for parts unknown."

"You didn't abandon your marriage?"

"There was nothing left to abandon. He betrayed my father and me."

"And broke your heart?"

This was more difficult than she'd feared. "He embarrassed me, humiliated me, but he didn't damage my heart because I never gave it to him. My father selected him for me, and, ever eager to please, I agreed. I thought I would learn to love him after a while, but it never happened."

"So you live on your teacher's salary and save money for your literacy center," he said noncommittally.

"Pretty conventional, isn't it? I'm not the princess I used to be. I haven't been to a society function in years, except to hit up people for contributions. But I like myself better now."

"No trips to Antibes?"

"No."

"What about Lud?"

"He doesn't exist."

"No?" The corners of his mouth twitched, whether with humor or condemnation, she couldn't tell.

"I'm sorry I misled—*lied*—to you. I hope you'll forgive me."

He started to speak, but she rushed on. "When I asked you to kiss me, I chose you because you were the sexiest man I'd met, and I knew instinctively that I could trust you with my fears, my needs...myself. I've never been so passionate since then, until recently," she added wistfully.

"When you stopped kissing me, insulted my womanliness, it hurt for a long, long time. Naively, I'd hoped you'd fall in love with me. That we could live happily ever after."

"Laurel—" His face was expressionless.

Determined to finish before the tears she was blinking back could break free, she said, "Now I understand that you saved us from a major mistake. We had no future together then."

"Do we have one now?" he asked gruffly.

"I love you, Wade, but I fought against recognizing it by blaming all my troubles on you. When we met again, I pretended to be the kind of woman I knew you'd never respect. I thought you hadn't changed, so I acted like I hadn't, either.

"I don't know if we have a future together. I just know I love you and have since I was seventeen. There's a lot that I don't know about you, but I do know that you can be kind and gentle, that you love Stella as much as I do, that you overcame a wretched childhood and grew into a responsible, caring man. You have looked out for me, taken care of me when I needed you to."

Forcing words past the knot of emotion that threatened to close her throat, she struggled to make him understand.

"I wanted you to know all these things so you won't keep on believing you aren't worthy of love, as I think your father made you believe. Or worthy of the love of a woman, as I think . . . I made you believe.

"There's too much history between us, that keeps you from loving me. But I know there's a woman out there especially for you. You *can* have the kind of loving relationship that Stella and Homer had. . . ."

He averted his gaze, staring silently at the roses.

Say something, she thought. *Say anything. Tell me to go to hell. You have a right to. Just please put an end to this.*

As he stood there, silent, her tenuous hope died. She gave up, now hoping only to salvage Stella's wish from disaster.

"It's okay," she said wearily. "You don't have to say anything. But please stand with me by those blasted roses and repeat the vows for Stella's sake. The words won't bind us. You can get on with your life, and I'll get on with mine."

He put on his sunglasses before turning to face her and speak wearily. "You and Stella stay here. I'll be back in two hours, and if you still want to, we'll say the vows." He walked up the path and out of her sight.

"Where did he go, dear?" Stella asked, frowning.

"I don't know." She repeated his instructions as she wheeled her aunt into the shade to wait.

Time dragged by while she kept up a cursory conversation with Stella and considered his devastating reaction to her confession. He wouldn't even say the simple words with her to please Stella.

He'd said he would return, but would he? He'd been so unwilling, so remote when he'd made that promise. For all she knew, he'd climbed into his car and headed out of town, while she waited in this romantic place, foolishly willing to pretend to be his bride because those few moments were all she'd ever have with Wade Taggart.

His time would be up in fifteen minutes. Then what? She and Stella could wait for a while, but for how long? When would she give up and admit that she'd been deserted?

"There he is," Stella crowed. "Oh, my, just look!"

She hardly recognized him.

His cheeks were clean-shaven, his hair had been cut in a conservative style. He'd traded his faded jeans and T-shirt for a sports coat, slacks and tie. If it weren't for his confident stride and sexy grin, she'd have taken him for a stranger. He carried a bouquet of summer flowers in one hand and had a large package tucked under the other arm.

Lord, he was gorgeous. Her heart danced erratically in her chest, leaving her speechless.

He'd come back! That unquenchable spark of hope sputtered to life in her again.

"Wade, dear, we were getting worried," Stella said, a vast understatement. "Who's that?" she asked, pointing toward a young woman who struggled down the path dragging a large black case on wheels.

"I'm the harpist," she announced. "Where should I set up?"

"Over there, in the shade," he instructed. "Play something romantic."

Captivated, she realized he'd gone all out, for a man who'd only agreed to play a part in a charade. That hopeful spark flamed. Maybe...

Maybe he only wanted to make the occasion as nice as possible for Stella, she cautioned.

He handed her the bouquet "I figured if I got roses, you'd think I stole them from the park," he teased, his eyes warm with humor—and something else she couldn't quite define. He caught her hand in one of his. "Come over here with me. There are some things *I* have to tell *you*."

Clutching the flowers as if they'd try to escape, she let him lead her to the other side of the flower bed.

"You aren't the only one who played a game of deceit, Laurel. I'm not living on the fringe, moving from one crummy job to another. I'm a business consultant. I make lots of money, though that was never my goal. I wanted respect, and I earned it by working my butt off since college. I worked relentlessly so my mind would be occupied. So I could keep from thinking about you, wondering where you were...what might have been if only we'd had a fair chance together.

"I guess I've always loved you, Laurel."

"Loved *me?* Always?" she whispered, unbelieving, unable to say more.

"As a kid I was jealous of you, resented you, competed with you for Homer and Stella's affection. But I loved you from the time I realized girls were different from boys." A crooked grin spread across his lips. Tears sheened his eyes, and he blinked to dispel them.

"I just never thought you'd love me," he said, his voice rough with emotion.

She'd never loved him more than at this moment.

"I want to marry you. Settle down. Trade in my big, lonely condo in Dallas for a home in Edgarville. I want to volunteer at your literacy center. I'll still have to travel some, but I want you to come with me when you can, and we'll explore the world together."

He paused and shifted his weight from foot to foot, as she stared at him in a speechless daze.

"This part isn't very romantic, but I've got to go to Athens in a couple of days to finish a business deal, but then—"

"I'll wait," she proclaimed, planting a quick, happy kiss on his lips. "I'm relieved that you have a real job. For a while, I thought you were an itinerant."

"When I close the deal, we'll honeymoon on a Greek island I know. Steep cliffs rising from the bluest water. White, sandy beaches. A romantic, old hotel with flowers cascading over the balconies. We'll dedicate ourselves to loving each other—and making love to each other."

"Oh, yes. Perfect."

"Hey, mister." The harpist's strident voice put an end to their interlude. "You paid me for three songs, and I've played them. If you want more music, you gotta pay more cash."

"Sure, sure." Never taking his gaze from Laurel, he waved his hand at the musician as if she were a pesky fly. "Coming right up.

"Ready, my love? Stella's waiting."

"Promise me something?"

"Anything short of the Taj Mahal."

"Don't ever become Mr. Comfortable. Oh, settle down some with me. But don't try to change yourself. I like my men—my *man*—with shaggy hair, beard stubble and a sense of adventure."

Grinning his agreement, he opened the large box he'd been carrying and lifted a pale pink caftan over her head, then held her flowers as the silk whispered down her body.

"A wedding dress!"

"I didn't think that clingy orange number was appropriate for this solemn occasion. This was the best I could do on short notice. Now, come on."

He signaled the harpist, who began plucking delicate notes from her instrument.

They stood before Stella, holding hands. He spoke solemnly of his love for Laurel, of his commitment for her alone, promising to stand beside her always as her husband, lover and best friend. He slipped an emerald engagement ring on the third finger of her left hand.

Laurel's turn came, and she spoke words from deep in her soul in a clear, soft voice, her heart near to bursting with excitement and the joy she'd never expected to share with Wade.

He whispered, "I'll always think of this as our true wedding. But I'll give you a wedding band when we get married officially. An informal marriage was fine for Stella and Homer, but I'm too conventional to skip the ceremony. I figure our children will appreciate it."

As Wade wrapped his arms around her, Stella hugged the red urn to her chest. "We did it, Homer. We knew we could!"

Laurel tossed her bouquet in the harpist's direction, then gave herself up to the kiss she'd waited for all her life.

* * * * *

Take 4 bestselling love stories FREE

Plus get a FREE surprise gift!

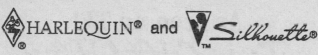

HARLEQUIN® and **Silhouette®**

are proud to present...

HERE COME THE GROOMS™

Four marriage-minded stories written by top
Harlequin and Silhouette authors!

Next month, you'll find:

A Practical Marriage	by Dallas Schulze
Marry Sunshine	by Anne McAllister
The Cowboy and the Chauffeur	by Elizabeth August
McConnell's Bride	by Naomi Horton

ADDED BONUS! In every edition of
Here Come the Grooms you'll find $5.00 worth
of coupons good for Harlequin and Silhouette
products.

On sale at your favorite Harlequin and Silhouette
retail outlet.

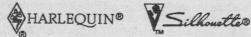

HARLEQUIN®   **Silhouette®**

HCTG896

As seen on TV!
Free Gift Offer

With a Free Gift proof-of-purchase from any Silhouette® book,
you can receive a beautiful cubic zirconia pendant.

This gorgeous marquise-shaped stone is a genuine cubic
zirconia—accented by an 18" gold tone necklace.

(Approximate retail value $19.95)

Send for yours today...
compliments of ▼ *Silhouette*®
™

To receive your free gift, a cubic zirconia pendant, send us one original proof-of-purchase, photocopies not accepted, from the back of any Silhouette Romance™, Silhouette Desire®, Silhouette Special Edition®, Silhouette Intimate Moments® or Silhouette Yours Truly™ title available in August, September or October at your favorite retail outlet, together with the Free Gift Certificate, plus a check or money order for $1.65 U.S./$2.15 CAN. (do not send cash) to cover postage and handling, payable to Silhouette Free Gift Offer. We will send you the specified gift. Allow 6 to 8 weeks for delivery. Offer good until October 31, 1996 or while quantities last. Offer valid in the U.S. and Canada only.

Free Gift Certificate

Name: _____

Address: _____

City: _____ State/Province: _____ Zip/Postal Code: _____

Mail this certificate, one proof-of-purchase and a check or money order for postage and handling to: SILHOUETTE FREE GIFT OFFER 1996. In the U.S.: 3010 Walden Avenue, P.O. Box 9077, Buffalo NY 14269-9077. In Canada: P.O. Box 613, Fort Erie, Ontario L2Z 5X3.

FREE GIFT OFFER   084-KMD
ONE PROOF-OF-PURCHASE
To collect your fabulous FREE GIFT, a cubic zirconia pendant, you must include this original proof-of-purchase for each gift with the properly completed Free Gift Certificate.

084-KMD

You're About to Become a *Privileged Woman*

Reap the rewards of fabulous free gifts and benefits with proofs-of-purchase from Silhouette and Harlequin books

Pages & Privileges™

It's our way of thanking you for buying our books at your favorite retail stores.

Harlequin and Silhouette— the most privileged readers in the world!

For more information about Harlequin and Silhouette's PAGES & PRIVILEGES program call the Pages & Privileges Benefits Desk: 1-503-794-2499

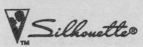

Silhouette®

SR-PP163